ADELINE

Adeline

THE MIRABELLE CHRONICLES BOOK FOUR

Sandi K. Wilson

SKW Publishing

Copyright © 2024 by Sandi K. Wilson
Cover Photography by www.istockphoto.com
Cover Design by SKW Publishing

ISBN 978-1-991296-20-7 Paperback
ISBN 978-1-991296-07-8 E-Book

All Scripture is in the Complete Jewish Bible unless otherwise stated.

All rights reserved. No part of this book may be reproduced in any manner whatsoever without written permission except in the case of brief quotations embodied in critical articles and reviews.

First Printing 2024, © SKW Publishing
www.skwpublishing.com

Adeline

Adeline is a rare beauty, her intelligence and curiosity matched only by her infectious humour and quick wit.

She has a strength that commands attention, yet beneath her confident exterior lies a hidden vulnerability she shares with few.

Her presence not only illuminates every room she enters but also ignites the spark of possibility in every heart she touches.

Facing a crossroads in her life, Adeline embarks on a journey spanning time and space, where mysteries unfold, adventure awaits and truths are finally found.

Dedication

To my darling daughter Stephanie,
My beautiful exuberant butterfly!
You possess a strength, determination and a wanderlust for life that I admire so greatly.
Thank you for your unconditional love, laughter and madness!

I utterly adore you,
Mothersaurus xxx

Acknowledgements

I wish to express my gratitude to all who have believed in me.

All those who have consistently prayed for me.

Those who encourage me when I'm ready to give up.

And for the role of Holy Spirit in this, and in all I seek to do.

My love always,

Sandi xx

Dear Reader

"Adeline"
A German name meaning:
Noble, nobility

With each book in The Mirabelle Chronicles, I aim to take real-life situations and weave them into stories that educate, inspire, and entertain. This particular book has been the most enjoyable to write!

While I've wrestled with balancing information and narrative, the journey of exploring both genetic and spiritual paths has been remarkable. My eldest daughter has been the inspiration behind this story. Together, we spent countless hours delving into our family tree, combing through archives, and painstakingly compiling information. The relatives we discovered, both near and distant, have become part of the story now in your hands.

It's no secret that being a person of faith in today's world can be a path filled with questions, doubts, fears, and concerns.

Yet faith is a core part of the daily lives of billions around the globe. For me, faith in Christ has been a beautiful yet challenging journey. Over the decades, the path has often been slippery, and at times incredibly painful. Learning that my heritage was tied to difficult cultural realities was hard to face, but the Lord faithfully walked me through it, leading me to true peace.

My hope for this story is that you not only find adventure but also great hope. We all struggle at times; we all fall. Life often brings more than we think we can bear, and we hold on to whatever we can to make it through. May that be the hand of hope and faith as you journey through these pages—and through life itself.

As always, may you be blessed on this journey.
Sandi xx

Prologue

Heavenly Whispers

The night was thick with silence, the kind that wrapped around the soul and amplified the whispers of the heart. Adeline stood at the edge of a vast, clifftop, the moon casting a silvery glow over the sea. The cool breeze tugged at her hair, carrying with it a sense of anticipation, as if the very air was charged with the promise of something extraordinary.

"Who are you?" Adeline whispered, her words echoing through the wind, a connection to the heavens.

Te Ata Whetu's eyes, reflecting the wisdom of millennia, locked onto Adeline's. "I am Te Ata Whetu, the dawn star," she began, her voice gentle yet filled with purpose. "I have been sent by Adonai – the one true Creator, your Papa, to walk with you through your journey into the past and your pilgrimage into the future."

Adeline felt a surge of energy, a connection forming deep within her. The feathers on Te Ata Whetu's Korowai (cloak) shimmered, reflecting the stories of ancestors and their journeys across the seas.

"Adeline, this Korowai is special," Te Ata Whetu continued. "Each feather carries the history and brilliance of your ancestors."

With Te Ata Whetu's guidance, Adeline's mind became clearer. Her sharp intellect and detective skills helped her begin to uncover the layers of her diverse background.

"Your heritage is rich and complex," Te Ata Whetu explained. "You are part Scottish Celt with their unique traditions, and part Viking from your birth father's lineage. Combined with your Maori roots, this creates a vivid picture of your unique identity."

As Te Ata Whetu spoke, the colours of her cloak—blues, greens, and golds—seemed to capture the essence of dawn and dusk. "The Celtic and Viking warriors and Tainui ancestors within you come together, shaping who you are."

Adeline felt the significance of her heritage and the blessing it brought. Te Ata Whetu's words showed her a path filled with challenges and discoveries, a journey that would test her in ways she had never imagined.

But with that knowledge came a deeper struggle. Adeline wrestled with her faith, facing doubts and seeking answers that had eluded her for so long. "You've been hurt by the church, by the very institution that was supposed to guide and nurture your faith," Te Ata Whetu acknowledged, her voice tinged with empathy. "You have many questions about faith, about the nature of the divine, and about your place in the grand tapestry of existence. But deep down, there's a spark in you, a flame that has not been extinguished, ready to be reignited."

"Your journey," Te Ata Whetu said firmly, "is one of self-discovery, rich culture, and balancing faith and questioning. Your Maori, Celtic, and Viking roots create a powerful heritage, guided by divine forces and the whispers of Papa."

The feathers on the Korowai continued to shine, each one telling a story and lighting the way for Adeline. As the vision began to fade and the fortress disappeared, Te Ata Whetu's final words echoed in Adeline's mind: "Adeline, I will help you find the courage to embrace your destiny and uncover the truths hidden in your heritage, if you allow me to?"

* * *

Adeline, found herself back in her room, startled and confused. The sudden shift from the mystical dream to the familiar surroundings of her bed left her disoriented.

The room, softly lit by the moonlight filtering through the curtains, felt both comforting and surreal. Her heart raced as the echoes of the vision and Te Ata Whetu's words lingered in her mind. The memory of her heavenly guide still hung in the air, leaving a strange, ethereal feeling.

Whether it had been a dream or a vision, the experience had left a lasting impression on her thoughts and emotions. In the quiet of the night, she pondered its significance and the connection she felt with Te Ata Whetu.

As Adeline settled back into the quiet of her room, she couldn't shake the feeling that the revelations weren't just confined to her dream. She wondered if she would have the courage to take this journey with Te Ata Whetu and uncover the truths that awaited her.

Quietly, she summoned a few words to pray; her words a soft murmur in the stillness of the night. "Papa," she whispered, her voice barely audible, "guide me, help me find the strength to walk this path, to embrace the journey you have set before me."

As she drifted back to sleep, the image of Te Ata Whetu's shimmering Korowai and the wisdom in her eyes lingered in her mind, a promise of the adventures and discoveries that lay ahead. The night held its breath, and the world waited, as Adeline took her first steps on the path to uncovering her destiny.

Contents

Adeline — v
Dedication — vii
Acknowledgements — ix
Dear Reader — xi
Prologue — xiii

1	The Seraphimite Order	1
2	The Weary Travellers	11
3	The Find	19
4	Qumran's Secrets	25
5	The Hidden Network	30
6	The Sicarii's Role	37
7	The Tunnel of Spirits	42
8	The Solo Quest	51
9	Adeline's Heartcry	57
10	The Longing	61
11	The Parables of Yeshua	67

12	The Letting Go	84
13	The Celts	87
14	The Vikings	95
15	Islands of the Sea	101
16	The Stone	107
17	Island Dream	112
18	Nani's Storytelling	122
19	Over the Centuries	126
20	The Mountain of Questions	131
21	The Norse Seafarers	138
22	The Gathering of Strength	144
23	The Call to Arms	153
24	Unearthed Memories	164
25	Threads of Destiny	169
26	Addie and Papa	174
27	The Revelation	184
28	The Unveiling	192

Epilogue   199
About The Author   205

1

The Seraphimite Order

Qumran 585 BCE

White hair gleaming in the lamplight, Rabbi Za'ir performed his ablutions with meticulous care, each movement deliberate and infused with reverence. The water was cool against his skin as he washed his hands according to the ancient rituals of his faith. He leaned over the basin, allowing the water to cleanse his face, the droplets slipping down like a thousand tiny blessings. With a practised hand, he reached for a cloth, patting his hands and face dry, feeling the weight of tradition settle upon his shoulders. This ritual, passed down through generations, was more than mere habit—it was a connection to his ancestors, a bridge between the past and the present that anchored him in a world that was ever-changing.

The room was dimly lit, the only source of illumination coming from the small oil lamp that flickered on the wooden bureau. Shadows danced on the rough stone walls, echoing the inner turmoil of the old rabbi's thoughts. The faint scent of olive oil mingled with the musty aroma of old parchment, a familiar and comforting blend that anchored him in the present. Each time he entered this space, the smells and sights greeted him like old friends, steady and unchanging, even as the world outside their enclave threatened to unravel.

Rabbi Za'ir carefully attached his phylacteries to his forehead and arm, feeling the worn leather straps bite into his skin, a reminder of the covenant he had sworn to uphold. The leather was smooth from years of use, the knots and loops familiar to his fingers as he secured them with the same precision he had for decades. These phylacteries, or tefillin, held within them fragments of scripture, the words of Adonai that had guided his people through trials and triumphs alike. He gathered his tallith, the fringes trailing like whispers of the past, and draped it over his shoulders. The tallith, with its tzitzit hanging like tendrils of history, was more than a garment; it was a mantle of responsibility, a symbol of his commitment to the faith and the people he served.

Taking a deep breath, he stepped out of the small chamber and into the predawn stillness. The air outside was crisp and clean, the freshness of the early morning filling his lungs with a renewed sense of purpose. Before him, the vast expanse of the Sea of Salt shimmered under the first light of dawn, its surface like a mirror reflecting the heavens above. The world seemed suspended between night and day, the sky tinged with the soft hues of violet and gold, as if the hand of Adonai Himself had painted the scene before him. Each morning brought with it a sense of rebirth, a reminder that no matter how dark the night, the light would always return.

As he made his way down the rocky path, the familiar crunch of sand and pebbles beneath his sandals provided a rhythm to his silent prayer. The path, worn smooth by the passage of many feet over the years, was a testament to the unwavering devotion of those who had walked it before him. Others had risen as well, their forms emerging like spectres from the shadows, men of faith and devotion who had dedicated their lives to the pursuit of purity and truth. These were the Seraphimites, a secretive order committed to preserving the sacred texts and teachings of their faith. They moved with purpose, descending the hill in silence, each step bringing them closer to their sacred ritual. Their silence was not born of fear, but of reverence; the stillness of the early morning was a time for reflection and connection with the divine.

The men gathered at the base of the hill, where the ground levelled and offered an unobstructed view of the horizon. They stood in a loose semicircle, facing east, where the sun would soon make its ascent over the distant mountains. Rabbi Za'ir joined them, his heart swelling with a sense of belonging, of being part of something ancient and unbroken. He could feel the presence of those who had come before, their spirits mingling with the living, as the continuity of their faith stretched across the ages.

With hands raised and fingers parted in the V shape, they began to recite the Shema, their voices rising in unison, deep and resonant. The ancient words rolled off their tongues like a river of sound, carrying with them the weight of countless generations who had spoken the same prayer. This was no mere recitation; it was an invocation of divine presence, a reminder of their duty to uphold the covenant made with their forefathers. Each word was like a thread, weaving together the fabric of their collective identity, binding them not only to each other but to the very essence of their faith.

"Sh'ma, Yisra'el! Adonai Eloheinu, Adonai echad translated: Hear, Isra'el! Adonai our God, Adonai is one; and you are to love Adonai your God with all your heart, all your being and all your resources…"

The sound of their prayer echoed across the water, reverberating off the cliffs and returning to them as a haunting refrain. It was as if the very earth was joining in their worship, amplifying their voices until they became one with the landscape. The sun, now fully risen, bathed them in its golden light, and for a moment, the world was filled with an ethereal glow, as though they were standing at the threshold of heaven itself. The interplay of light and shadow seemed to transform the men, their figures silhouetted against the sky, into something otherworldly —beings suspended between the mortal and the divine.

The words of the Shema, drawn from the sacred scrolls, filled the air with a sense of sanctity and devotion. Each syllable was a bridge between the earthly and the divine, a testament to their unwavering faith. Rabbi Za'ir's voice, deep and steady, mingled with the others, creating a symphony of devotion that resonated in his very soul. In this moment, all his doubts and fears melted away, replaced by a profound sense of peace. The weight of the world, the responsibilities he carried, felt lighter in the presence of such unity and faith.

As the prayer came to an end, the men lowered their hands, their eyes still fixed on the horizon where the sky met the sea. There was a moment of stillness, a shared breath, as they absorbed the significance of what they had just spoken. The Shema was more than a prayer; it was a declaration of their identity, a reaffirmation of their bond with the Creator. Each time they recited these words, they renewed their commitment to the path laid out before them, a path that was often fraught with challenges but also illuminated by the light of divine guidance.

Slowly, they turned and began the ascent back up the hill, their footsteps synchronized in a silent rhythm. The air was filled with the scents of the desert, the dry earth mingling with the faint fragrance of wild herbs that clung to the rocky slopes. These herbs, resilient and tenacious, seemed to symbolize the enduring spirit of the people who called this harsh land home. The sun continued its climb, casting long shadows that stretched like fingers across the landscape, as if reaching out to touch the sacred ground beneath their feet.

The group of men entered a modest building near the summit, its stone walls blending seamlessly with the rugged terrain. Inside, the room was fitted with scrolls, tables, and chairs, each piece of furniture arranged with precision and care. Many oil lamps had been lit, their flickering flames casting a warm glow that softened the harsh lines of the stone walls. The room exuded a sense of purpose and serenity, a sanctuary where the divine and the mundane met in the delicate dance of transcription.

The men took their places, settling at the tables where the tools of their trade awaited them. The quills, sharpened to perfection, lay beside inkwells filled with the precious ink they used to inscribe the holy texts. The scrolls, made of carefully prepared parchment, were unrolled before them, their surfaces smooth and ready to receive the sacred words. The parchment itself was a testament to the care and dedication of the scribes; it had been meticulously treated and prepared, each sheet representing countless hours of work.

Rabbi Za'ir paused at the entrance, his gaze sweeping over the room. This was their sanctuary, a place where they could immerse themselves in the divine task of transcribing the Torah. Everything here was dedicated to the preservation of their faith, from the style of writing to the precise margins of the scrolls. Even the seals that would be placed upon the completed scrolls were crafted with the utmost care, a final act of devotion before the words were hidden away. The room, though simple, carried an air of solemnity, a sacred space where the physical act of writing became an act of worship.

He offered a silent prayer of thanks for the Torah, the foundation of their lives and the light that guided their steps. The Torah was more than a set of laws and teachings; it was the living word of Adonai, a source of wisdom and guidance that had shaped their people for generations. To be entrusted with its preservation was a responsibility that weighed heavily on the rabbi, but it was also a source of immense pride.

With a sense of solemnity, Rabbi Za'ir began to remove his outer garments, stripping down to his undergarment in preparation for the mikvah. The ceremonial pool, carved into the rock outside, was fed by a natural spring, its waters cold and clear. It was here that they would cleanse themselves before engaging in the holy work of writing the scrolls. The mikvah was more than a ritual cleansing; it was a moment of spiritual renewal, a purification that prepared the scribes to handle the sacred texts with the reverence they deserved.

As Rabbi Za'ir descended into the mikvah, the chill of the water was a shock to his system, but it also served to focus his mind, to wash away the doubts and fears that had crept into his thoughts. The water, cool and invigorating, seemed to seep into his very being, washing away the fatigue of his years and the weight of his responsibilities. He submerged himself fully, the water closing over his head like a blanket of peace. For a moment, he lingered beneath the surface, allowing the silence to envelop him, to drown out the noise of the world.

But even in this sanctuary, the weight of his responsibilities pressed down on him. The decision they had made, to hide the sacred scrolls and precious artifacts in the caves of Qumran, was a burden he carried alone. What if they were discovered? What if the secrets they had vowed to protect were revealed to the world before the appointed time? These questions gnawed at him, even as he tried to push them from his mind.

He surfaced, gasping for air, and felt the doubts slip away as the water cascaded off his body. The decision had been made, and there was no turning back. The Seraphimites had agreed unanimously, understanding the gravity of their situation and the necessity of preserving their sacred knowledge. He dressed quickly, wrapping himself in the tallith once more, and returned to the writing room where his fellow Seraphimites awaited him. The sight of them, gathered in silence, their faces set in determined focus, reassured him. He was not alone in this task; they were bound together by their faith and their shared commitment.

Today, he would be writing the holy and majestic name of Adonai – YHWH. The name was so sacred, it could only be written in one specific way, each stroke of the quill a prayer in itself. The weight of this responsibility settled on his shoulders like a mantle, but it was a weight he bore with pride and reverence. Writing the name of Adonai was not just a task; it was an act of devotion, a moment where the scribe became a conduit for the divine. The strokes had to be perfect, the ink flawless, and the intent pure. Any mistake would require the entire parchment to be discarded, a costly and painful reminder of the gravity of their work.

The men worked in silence, their focus absolute as they carefully inscribed the sacred texts. Time seemed to stand still in the room, the hours slipping by unnoticed as they lost themselves in the rhythm of their work. Each word they wrote was an offering, each scroll a testament to their unwavering faith. The room was filled with the sound of quills scratching against parchment, a quiet, almost hypnotic sound that underscored the sanctity of their task.

As the hours passed, Rabbi Za'ir found himself reflecting on the path that had led him to this moment. He had been a young man when he first joined the Seraphimites, full of zeal and a desire to serve. Over the years, he had seen many come and go, but the core of their order had remained steadfast, committed to the preservation of the sacred texts. They had witnessed the rise and fall of kings, the destruction of temples, and the scattering of their people, yet their mission had never wavered. The Torah was the lifeblood of their faith, and they were its guardians.

When the day drew to a close, the men hurried to roll and carefully store the completed scrolls in pottery amphorae. The lids were sealed with wax, the scrolls protected from the elements and the ravages of time. Together, they walked the scrolls up to a prepared cave, where they would be hidden away, safe from prying eyes, until the appointed time when they would be discovered and their secrets revealed. The journey to the cave was a solemn procession, each man carrying his burden with a sense of reverence. The cave, carved into the side of the mountain, was a place of refuge, a hidden sanctuary where their work would be safe from the world.

Rabbi Za'ir stood at the entrance of the cave, watching as the men placed the amphorae in their final resting place. The sun had begun its descent, casting a warm golden light over the desert landscape. The scene was almost surreal, the golden light bathing the desert in a glow that felt both comforting and otherworldly. He congratulated the men for their speed and haste in the delivery of the scrolls, knowing that time was of the essence. Yet, even as he spoke, a part of him wondered how long they would have until their secrets were uncovered. The knowledge they had preserved was powerful, and in the wrong hands, it could be used to devastating effect.

The task completed, the men returned to their quarters, their bodies weary from the day's labour but their spirits buoyed by the knowledge that they had done their part to preserve the sacred texts. The sense of accomplishment was palpable; they had fulfilled their duty, ensuring that the wisdom of the Torah would endure, even in the darkest of times. After their evening rituals and prayers, they each found their way to their sleeping mats, and as the darkness of the desert night closed in, they fell into a deep and dreamless slumber.

But even as they slept, the scrolls they had hidden away whispered their secrets to the silent stones, waiting for the day when they would once again see the light of day. The caves of Qumran, with their hidden treasures, would remain untouched for centuries, a silent witness to the faith and devotion of the Seraphimites. And when the appointed time came, the world would discover the depths of their sacrifice and the power of the words they had preserved.

2

The Weary Travellers

Exhausted and weary, the group of Shamar, Hezekiah, Zidkiyah, Haggai, and Zechariah traversed the desert; the Qumran mountain range loomed ahead, its jagged peaks silhouetted against the fading light of day. The vast expanse of sand and rock stretched out before them, a harsh and unforgiving landscape that had tested their endurance and resolve for many days. The sun dipped below the horizon, casting long shadows across the rugged terrain, and the coolness of evening began to settle in, offering a brief respite from the relentless heat of the day. The sky, a canvas of deepening purples and oranges, seemed to mirror the exhaustion and determination etched into the faces of the travellers.

Tired and with the settlement of the Seraphimites in sight, they quickened their pace, eager to find respite for the night. The knowledge that shelter and food awaited them spurred their tired bodies forward, their minds clinging to the hope of a brief reprieve from the trials of their journey. The Seraphimites were known for their hospitality and devotion, a brotherhood that had long dedicated themselves to the preservation of sacred texts and ancient knowledge. To the weary travellers, this settlement was more than just a place to rest—it was a sanctuary, a beacon of hope in the desolate wilderness.

Arriving just as the sun's last rays kissed the horizon, the men were greeted by Rabbi Za'ir, a venerable figure with a long, flowing beard that mirrored the wisdom etched in his eyes. His presence was both comforting and commanding, a living embodiment of the spiritual strength and resilience that defined the Seraphimites. His robes, simple yet dignified, swayed gently in the evening breeze as he approached the travellers, his gaze filled with warmth and understanding.

Zechariah, the head of the group, approached Rabbi Za'ir with a deep sense of respect. As was the custom among those who walked the paths of righteousness, he kissed the Rabbi on both cheeks, a gesture of reverence and brotherhood. Their eyes met, and in that brief exchange, the hardships of the journey were acknowledged. Words were unnecessary; the bond between them, forged by shared faith and purpose, was stronger than any physical greeting.

The donkeys, burdened with supplies, stood patiently nearby, their sides heaving from the exertion of the day. These humble beasts of burden had carried not only provisions but also the weight of the travellers' mission—a mission shrouded in secrecy and fraught with significance. Rabbi Za'ir, recognizing the fatigue etched on the men's faces, assured them with a gentle smile, "No problems, my friends. Our men will take care of unpacking the donkeys for you." His words were like a balm to their weary souls, offering them the chance to rest without worry.

Gratitude filled Zechariah's tired eyes as the weight of their burdens was lifted, even if just for a moment. He nodded in thanks, the simple act of relinquishing control a rare luxury in their current lives. The travellers watched as several young Seraphimites, their faces alight with youthful energy, approached the donkeys with practised efficiency. The young men moved quickly but carefully, their hands deftly untying the ropes and unloading the precious cargo. It was clear that this community operated as a well-honed unit, each member playing a vital role in the smooth functioning of their daily life.

Guided by a few of the Seraphimites, the men were led to a room within the settlement. The stone walls of the building were cool to the touch, a welcome contrast to the harshness of the desert outside. Inside, the room was modest yet warm, a space where simplicity and comfort coexisted. Woven mats covered the stone floor, and a low table, surrounded by cushions, occupied the centre of the room. A simple meal awaited them, and the aroma of freshly baked bread mingled with the scent of desert herbs, filling the air with a warmth that reached beyond physical sustenance. The food, though humble, was prepared with care and reverence, a reflection of the Seraphimites' devotion to their faith and their guests.

The other men in the group had already settled in, their hunger satiated by the hospitality of the Seraphimites. Zechariah joined his companions, and the room buzzed with a quiet camaraderie. Their weariness was momentarily forgotten as they shared a meal, the simple act of breaking bread fostering a sense of unity that went beyond the physical. The bread, warm and soft, was passed from hand to hand, a symbol of the shared journey that had brought them together. The water, cool and refreshing, washed away the dust of the road, rejuvenating their spirits.

Amidst the flickering light of oil lamps, the men spoke minimally, each lost in his thoughts, contemplating the task that lay ahead. The soft glow of the lamps cast dancing shadows on the walls, creating an atmosphere of introspection and quiet reflection. Each man carried within him a deep sense of purpose, a knowledge that the journey they were on was no ordinary one. The sacred texts they sought to protect, the ancient knowledge they sought to preserve—these were more than just relics of the past. They were the lifeblood of their people, the foundation upon which their faith was built.

After the meal, the Seraphimites ushered the tired travellers to their accommodations. Each man found a simple cot, a welcome haven for their weary bodies. The night air outside carried a serene calm, punctuated only by the distant sounds of the desert—the soft rustling of the wind through the dunes, the occasional cry of a nocturnal creature. The tranquillity of the night offered a stark contrast to the challenges of the day, allowing the men to finally relax, if only for a few hours.

As the men settled into their quarters, the plan unfolded in their minds, its intricate details echoing through their thoughts. Tomorrow, at sunrise after morning prayers, the carefully crafted scheme would be set into motion. They knew that the path they were on was fraught with danger and uncertainty, but their faith in the divine plan gave them the strength to carry on.

With a sense of purpose, Shamar, Hezekiah, Zidkiyah, Haggai, and Zechariah drifted into a deep, dreamless sleep, anticipating the challenges and revelations that awaited them with the dawn. The settlement of the Seraphimites, nestled in the shadows of the Qumran mountain range, held the key to unlocking the mysteries that had been veiled for centuries.

***

The first light of dawn painted the desert sky with hues of pink and gold, the men rose from their cots. The morning air was cool and crisp, carrying with it the promise of a new day. The essence of the morning was infused with quiet anticipation and determination. They moved through their morning prayers and rituals with a sense of urgency, knowing that the day ahead held a significant undertaking. The prayers, whispered in unison, rose like a chorus of hope, a plea for guidance and protection as they prepared to embark on their sacred mission.

Several Seraphimites joined them, their faces reflecting both seriousness and an underlying joy and peace. These men, like their visitors, understood the gravity of the task ahead. They too had dedicated their lives to the preservation of the sacred, and the prospect of fulfilling their purpose filled them with a quiet but resolute joy. The Seraphimites, keepers of ancient wisdom and guardians of sacred artifacts, stood beside the group, ready to embark on this journey that held the promise of unveiling hidden truths.

In the soft glow of the morning light, the men gathered for a brief meeting. Rabbi Za'ir, the venerable leader of the

Seraphimites, addressed them with a steady voice that carried the weight of centuries of tradition. "Today, my friends, we venture into the footsteps of prophecy. The scrolls of Jeremiah and the Maccabees guide us to specific locations where the treasure must be buried." His words, though simple, were charged with a sense of destiny. Each man in the room knew that they were about to become part of a story much larger than themselves, a story that had been written long before they were born.

The locations within the compound had been previously marked out for the ardous task of digging, so that the treasure engraved upon the copper scroll, could be recorded for posterity. Armed with their tools, the men, with reverence and humility, went about digging in the parched ground to bury this most valuable and holy treasure.

The men reconvened and Rabbi Za'ir continued, "And now, the final piece that must be collected and delivered to the community is the most significant of all—the Tabernacle of Moshe (Moses). It is not only a treasure of material wealth but a symbol of our heritage and faith." The mention of the Tabernacle brought a hush over the group. The Tabernacle of Moshe was more than just a relic; it was the embodiment of their faith, a physical representation of the covenant between their people and the divine.

The group listened intently, understanding the weight of their mission. The Tabernacle of Moshe, a sacred structure with historical and spiritual significance, was the linchpin in their quest. Its retrieval would not only secure the community's future but also preserve a vital piece of their shared history. The men knew that what they were about to do would resonate through the generations, a legacy that would endure long after they were gone.

With the sun ascending in the sky, casting a warm glow over the desert landscape, the men and the chosen Seraphimites set out on their journey. As they walked to the location marked in the sacred texts, the weight of their mission hung in the air. The silence of the desert was broken only by the soft sounds of their footsteps and the occasional whisper of the wind, as if the very earth was holding its breath in anticipation.

With deep reverence and profound honour, the group of men approached the sacred Tabernacle, fully aware of its delicate condition. Each man carefully lifted the Tabernacle, recognizing it not only as a tangible artifact but as a vessel carrying the essence of their shared history and the promise of a future destiny. The wood, though aged, was sturdy; the linen curtains, though faded, still held the intricate patterns that spoke of a time long past. This time, they chose to transport it on a cart, pulled by two donkeys, a decision made with great consideration for the Tabernacle's fragility.

The group traversed the desert landscape with the cart, the men maintained a solemn atmosphere, contemplating the sacred nature of their cargo. The Tabernacle, composed of wood, linen curtains, and skins from rams and goats, held within it layers of spiritual and cultural significance. The journey itself became a manifestation of their commitment to preserving the sanctity of their heritage. Each turn of the wheels, each step of the donkeys, was a step closer to fulfilling their sacred duty.

By the time they reached the compound again at sundown in Qumran, the younger members of the community emerged to assist with unloading the cart. The setting sun bathed the scene in a golden light, casting long shadows that danced across the ground as the men worked together to carefully extract the heavy Tabernacle. Extracting the sacred artifact required meticulous planning and careful maneuvering, ensuring that every element, from the wooden structure to the intricately woven curtains, was handled with the utmost care. The young men, though inexperienced, moved with a reverence and care that belied their years, understanding the significance of the moment.

The members of the community, keenly aware of the significance of this moment, acknowledged the readiness of the hiding place with a shared understanding. It was as if the very stones of the cave had been waiting for this moment, a place of refuge for the sacred artifact, hidden away from the eyes of the world until the time was right.

As the final stone was placed to seal the entrance of the cave, a profound sense of accomplishment washed over them. They had done their part; the rest was in the hands of the divine.

Making their way back to the settlement, the stars began to emerge, one by one, in the clear desert sky. The night was still, the silence of the desert a stark contrast to the weight of the task they had just completed. Yet within that silence was a sense of peace, a knowledge that they had fulfilled their duty to their people and their faith. The journey had been long, and the path had been difficult, but they had persevered. And now, as they looked up at the stars, they knew that their story would continue, written in the heavens above and in the hearts of those who would come after them.

3

The Find

Qumran, Modern Day

In the heart of a Qumran archaeological site, Adeline, known as Addie, found herself on a mission of historical significance. Tasked with aiding a team led by Tim Fields, a seasoned archaeologist and ex-detective, in excavating the long-sought treasure outlined in *The Copper Scroll*—a centuries-old copper document discovered in the caves of the Qumran ranges—Addie stumbled upon revelations that left the team astounded. However, as excitement mounted, so did the challenges, primarily the daunting task of safeguarding their discovery from prying eyes—be it the media, the press, or shadowy figures with sinister motives.

Tim, ever vigilant, scanned the site with a sharp eye, his detective instincts still as keen as ever.

"We need to be careful," he cautioned, his voice low but firm. "This find could change everything, but it also makes us a target."

Adeline, with an intense gaze that saw beyond the ordinary, pushed her tortoiseshell glasses up her nose, wiped away perspiration, and, at a loss for words, shared a joyous laugh with her spirited mother, Alexandria.

"I can't believe it, Eema. I can't believe it."

Curious, Alexandria inquired, "What have you found, Addie?"

"Come take a look. It speaks for itself." Addie's smile beckoned her mother closer.

As Alexandria observed the excavation site, she gasped, covering her mouth in disbelief.

"It can't be!"

Tim joined them, his brow furrowed in concentration as he studied the find.

"Let's dig a little more and then see if we can start to gently remove this," he suggested.

Under his experienced guidance, the team carefully loosened the soil, revealing more of the artifact. Adeline's delight erupted as the relic came fully into view.

"It is, Eema. It really is!"

Mother and daughter embraced, laughing and jumping in tandem. Papa, grinning, observed his jubilant daughters. One of history's long-sought treasures had finally been unearthed, but the challenge now was to safeguard the discovery until their next steps were solidified.

Tim, with a mix of excitement and caution, started enacting stringent measures to secure the newly found object.

"We need to lock this site down immediately," he instructed the team. "No one gets in or out without clearance."

Adeline, after staring at the artifact for what felt like hours, turned to her Papa with a question.

"Why me, Papa? I'm not an archaeologist, I'm lacking direct expertise. I've only absorbed knowledge from TV series, documentaries, and my insatiable curiosity. Why entrust me with finding one of history's greatest mysteries? I'm no Indiana Jones —or Josh Gates!"

They shared a laugh at the comparison. Papa responded, "Adeline, you sought mystery, intrigue, adventure, and the uncovering of lost historical objects. This is just the beginning, my daughter. So, I ask, why *not* you?"

Grateful for the adventure yet concerned about public perception, Adeline expressed her worries to Papa.

"Ah, now we're getting to the heart of the matter, Adeline. You needn't concern yourself with others' perceptions, only yours and mine."

Papa, with raised eyebrows and a comical face, added a touch of humor to the conversation, a trait Adeline loved about Him— the divine being with a wild sense of humor!

Tim, observing the interaction from a distance, smiled knowingly. He had seen enough in his career to know that sometimes the most unexpected people are the key to unraveling the greatest mysteries.

"So, what do we do now?" Adeline asked, turning back to the task at hand.

Tim stepped forward, his voice steady and reassuring. "We keep digging. This is only the beginning. Who knows, we might uncover an entire town of treasures and artifacts that could shake the world or turn these so-called 'professionals' grey overnight!"

Papa laughed heartily, doing a jig, and pulled Adeline into a spontaneous dance, both filled with laughter and merriment.

In a manner reminiscent of Gandalf and Frodo Baggins, Adeline and Papa formed an unconventional yet formidable team—minus the long hair and pipe, but brimming with camaraderie and a shared sense of adventure.

As the laughter settled, Mirabelle, the leader of the Army, approached, her eyes twinkling with excitement.

"Addie, what have you found?" she asked, her curiosity barely contained.

Before Addie could respond, Claudine and Leo, her sister and brother-in-law, joined them.

"We heard the commotion," Claudine said, a knowing smile on her face. "What's all the excitement about?"

Addie beamed at her family, the joy of the discovery evident. "We've found something incredible. I can't explain it, you have to see for yourself."

Tim, always the professional, added, "It's beyond anything we expected, but it's crucial we handle this carefully. This site has more secrets to reveal."

Davvie, their younger brother, looked on with wide eyes. "This is all new to me," he admitted. "Dreams, visions, and now this? It's a bit overwhelming."

Alexandria, passionate about her family, faith, Israel, and adventure, placed a comforting hand on Davvie's shoulder.

"You'll get used to it, Davvie. We're all on this journey together."

Drew, her husband, emerged from the nearby tunnels with Petrucia, their foremother and member of the Cloud of Witnesses, Moshe, the supposed tour guide who was actually a celestial angel, and Jeanne d'Arc, the maiden warrior. Drew's face lit up when he saw the gathered group.

"What's all the excitement?"

Addie pointed to the find. "We've discovered one of the treasures from the Copper Scroll. It's beyond words."

Jeanne d'Arc, with a warrior's instinct, studied the site. "It looks like the beginning of something monumental."

Petrucia nodded, her ancient wisdom evident. "Indeed, but why has Papa brought us all here now?"

Papa had stood back and was watching the group as they chatted back and forth. The group fell silent, pondering the question.

It was Mirabelle who voiced what they were all thinking, smiling at her beloved Papa. "Papa has his reasons. Perhaps it's not just about the find, but about what we're meant to do with it."

Papa grinned. He knew his daughter well.

Adeline, still grappling with the enormity of the discovery and her role in it, looked at her family, Tim, and the celestial beings surrounding her.

"So, what's our next move?"

Tim, with a reassuring smile, said, "We continue together, trusting in Papa's plan. This is only the beginning of our adventure."

The group nodded, united in purpose. As they prepared to delve deeper into the mysteries of Qumran, Adeline couldn't help but feel a surge of determination. She glanced at Papa, the question still lingering in her mind.

"Why me?" she thought.

Papa's gentle laughter echoed in her heart. "Why not you, Adeline? Why not you?"

With a renewed sense of purpose, Adeline embraced the journey ahead. Yet, as she looked at the ancient artifact glinting under the moonlight, a chilling thought crossed her mind.

What if this discovery was only the beginning of something far more dangerous?

She turned to her family, Tim, and the companions, her voice barely a whisper.

"What have we truly uncovered here?"

4

Qumran's Secrets

The sun-drenched landscape of Qumran bore witness to a moment of profound significance as the excavation team, led by Tim Fields, unearthed a treasure not foreseen in their wildest imaginations. Adeline, with her analytical mind and penchant for mystery, stood at the heart of the discovery.

As the layers of soil gave way to history's embrace, the team uncovered not a key but a relic of unparalleled importance — Moshe's Tabernacle. The air seemed to shimmer with the weight of the revelation, and the team, momentarily suspended in awe, marvelled at the relic that transcended time itself.

Tim Fields, his eyes wide with amazement, approached Adeline. "This is beyond anything we could have imagined," he exclaimed. "Moshe's Tabernacle, a piece of history lost to the ages, has emerged from the shadows. The Copper Scroll's secrets are more profound than we dared to dream."

Adeline, carefully touching the relic with her hands, felt a connection to the ancient past coursing through her. The tabernacle, a sacred space that once housed the presence of Adonai, now lay exposed to the light of day after centuries of obscurity.

This sacred structure, an embodiment of ancient craftsmanship and divine connection, unfolded before the team like a time-worn tapestry. Woven from intricately spun textiles, the tabernacle bore the marks of antiquity. The fabric, miraculously preserved through the ages, spoke of a knowledge and artistry that surpassed the comprehension of the modern world.

The question of the tabernacle's age hung in the air, a mystery that added layers to the unfolding narrative. Tim, the seasoned archaeologist, theorised, "This structure could be thousands of years old, dating back to the era of Moshe himself. The preservation is remarkable, and it raises questions about ancient techniques that have eluded our understanding."

As the team at Qumran carefully unfolded and reassembled the Tabernacle of Moshe, a structure thought lost to history, they were met with a sight that transcended their wildest expectations. The sun's rays danced upon the ancient fabric, illuminating the intricate craftsmanship that had endured the ravages of time.

The Tabernacle stood in its full glory, a large rectangular structure with a frame made of acacia wood, the beams and poles fitted together with bronze clasps that gleamed faintly in the sunlight. The wood, despite its age, was remarkably preserved, with a deep, rich colour that spoke of its ancient origins. Each beam was meticulously carved, the surface worn smooth from centuries of use and exposure.

The structure was covered by multiple layers of fabric and animal skins, each with its own unique texture and colour, adding to the Tabernacle's otherworldly appearance: the outermost layer was made of tanned animal skins, possibly dolphin or badger, that had weathered the passage of time with surprising resilience. These skins, once a protective barrier against the elements, had faded to a muted greyish-brown, their surfaces toughened but still supple, as if imbued with an ancient preservation technique lost to modern understanding.

Beneath this outer layer was a thick curtain woven from goat hair, its texture coarse and rugged. The curtain, once a deep black, had lightened over the centuries to a dark charcoal, with strands of the fabric still tightly woven, providing an added layer of protection and insulation.

The innermost covering was crafted from fine linen, still vibrant with the colours of blue, purple, and scarlet, though softened by time. This layer was adorned with embroidered cherubim, their forms woven with such skill that they seemed to be in motion, their wings outstretched in eternal guardianship. The colours, though slightly faded, retained a sense of divine artistry, hinting at the sacredness of the space within.

Inside the Tabernacle, the air felt different – cooler, almost reverent, as if the very atmosphere acknowledged the sanctity of the space. The walls, lined with more finely woven linen, were embroidered with repeating patterns of cherubim, creating an ethereal sense of being in the presence of the divine.

The light within the Tabernacle was dim and soft, filtering through the layers of fabric in muted hues, creating a serene, almost dreamlike ambience. The ground beneath their feet was covered with the same linen, worn but intact, its intricate designs telling stories of ancient rituals and worship.

The space inside the Tabernacle was imbued with an overwhelming sense of history and sacredness. The air was thick with the scent of ancient incense, a lingering aroma of frankincense, myrrh, and other sacred spices, as if the prayers of the past had left an indelible mark on the very fabric of the structure.

As the team stood within the Tabernacle, they were enveloped by the weight of its history. The delicate interplay of light and shadow, the intricate patterns and textures of the fabrics, and the palpable sense of the divine presence all combined to create an atmosphere that was both awe-inspiring and humbling. It was a space that seemed to exist outside of time, a sacred relic that had survived the ages to tell its story.

Adeline, her hands gently tracing the embroidered cherubim, felt a profound connection to the past. The Tabernacle was a reminder of the enduring connection between the ancient and the spiritual, a bridge between the temporal and the eternal.

***

Tim addressed the group, "The discovery of Moshe's tabernacle is unprecedented. We stand on the threshold of history, and our actions will shape the narrative for generations to come. Adeline, your unique insights have brought us to this moment, but we must now consider the ethical implications of further excavation."

Adeline, ever attuned to the atmospheric currents, understood the gravity of the situation. The heavenly beings, silent witnesses to the unfolding events, seemed to guide the team toward a decision that respected the sanctity of the discovery.

"The secrets of Qumran are vast, and this tabernacle holds the key to unlocking a chapter lost in time," Tim continued. "However, our responsibility is not only to uncover history but to ensure its preservation for future generations. Let us proceed with caution, seeking wisdom through prayer."

As the team deliberated, the relics of the past whispered tales of a bygone era, urging the archaeologists to tread with reverence. The journey into Qumran's secrets had taken an unexpected turn, and the unfolding chapters promised a delicate dance between discovery and preservation, guided by both the tangible and the celestial.

5

The Hidden Network

The dim glow of their lanterns cast long shadows on the walls, flickering over ancient inscriptions and the rough-hewn stone that spoke of a time long past. Every step echoed with the ghosts of those who had walked these tunnels centuries before, the Sicarii who had built this labyrinthine world beneath the earth to protect what they held dear.

Papa led the way, his steps sure and confident, as though he had walked these tunnels many times before. The air grew cooler as they descended deeper, the silence punctuated only by the soft sounds of their footsteps and the occasional distant drip of water. The group was tense with anticipation, the significance of their journey becoming more apparent with each passing moment.

"Papa," Drew began, his voice hushed in the cavernous space, "how did the Sicarii manage to build something so extensive without the Romans ever discovering it?"

Papa paused, turning to face the group, his eyes gleaming with a mix of pride and sorrow. "The Sicarii were more than just rebels. They were master builders, engineers, and strategists. They knew that their survival depended not just on their strength, but on their ability to outthink their enemies. These tunnels were their lifeline, their sanctuary. They were careful, patient, and above all, determined."

Jeanne, who had been silent for much of the journey, spoke up, her voice tinged with awe. "It's incredible. The craftsmanship, the scale of it all... they weren't just hiding. They were living, thriving even, right under the noses of their oppressors."

Petrucia, examining the walls closely as they moved, added, "And they weren't alone. The Seraphimites in Qumran, the keepers of the Dead Sea Scrolls, they must have known about this. There are symbols here—shared markings that suggest a collaboration, or at least a mutual understanding."

The tunnel they were following began to widen, and soon they found themselves standing at the entrance to a large chamber. The ceiling arched high above them, supported by stone pillars carved with intricate patterns that seemed almost alive in the flickering light. It was a grand hall, far more sophisticated than anything they had seen so far.

"This must be the heart of it," Alex whispered, her voice filled with reverence. "The central point where everything connects."

Indeed, as they spread out to explore, they found passageways branching off in all directions, each leading to different parts of the subterranean complex. Some tunnels were narrow and winding, while others were broad enough to accommodate groups of people. The scale was overwhelming, the sheer ingenuity of it all stunning them into silence.

As the group continued their exploration of the tunnels, they became increasingly aware of the duality of the space they inhabited. The passageways carried the marks of both the Sicarii's rugged determination and the Seraphimites' meticulous care. Where the walls bore the rough chiselling of a hurried hand, they would soon smooth out, revealing the careful work of the Seraphimites. This contrast fascinated the group, prompting them to delve deeper into the mysterious alliance between these two vastly different sects.

"Papa," Alexandria asked, breaking the silence as they entered a broader chamber, "why would the Sicarii and the Seraphimites work together? They seem so... different."

Papa paused, looking around at the walls adorned with symbols and inscriptions that had been carefully preserved despite the passage of centuries. "They were different," he began, his voice echoing softly through the chamber. "But in the face of annihilation, they found common ground. Both groups believed in the survival of their people, their faith, and their heritage. And they knew that the Romans posed an existential threat to all of it."

Jeanne, examining the inscriptions more closely, noted, "These markings are not just decorative. They seem to be a blend of Sicarii and Seraphimite symbols, almost like a shared code."

Petrucia, who had been studying a scroll she had found in the alcove, looked up with a revelation. "The Seraphimites were not just peaceful scribes. They were keepers of knowledge, and they believed that their writings were a means of preserving the truth of their faith. The Sicarii, on the other hand, saw the Romans as a direct threat to that truth. It makes sense that they would collaborate to protect something that was sacred to both of them."

Just as the group began to digest this new revelation, Addie spoke up. Her voice was clear, cutting through the weighty silence. "So, the Seraphimites provided the knowledge, the writings, and the Sicarii provided the protection? It's like they each had a piece of the puzzle to keep their world from falling apart."

Papa smiled warmly at Addie, pleased with her insight. "Exactly, Addie. They were different in many ways, but they shared a vision of preserving what was sacred to them. In times of great peril, even the most unlikely allies can find a way to work together."

Claudine, who had been quietly observing everything, finally voiced her thoughts. "It's strange, isn't it? To think that the Sicarii, who were so bent on fighting, and the Seraphimites, who were dedicated to peace, could come together like this. It's almost... poetic."

Davvie, who had been trailing behind the group and still trying to wrap his head around the entire situation, finally spoke up, his tone laced with a mix of bewilderment and amusement. "I still can't believe I'm here. I mean—what do I know about ancient tunnels and secret alliances? This is something out of a movie, not real life!"

The group chuckled, the tension easing slightly with Davvie's light-hearted remark. Addie turned to him with a reassuring smile. "You might not understand, Davvie, but you're also a part of this team. We all bring something different to the table, just like the Sicarii and the Seraphimites."

Davvie nodded, still a bit overwhelmed but visibly comforted by Addie's words. "Thanks, Addie. I guess you're right. This is just... a lot to take in, and I have no idea what I will be contributing to this team."

As the group ventured deeper into the chamber, they discovered what appeared to be a small library, with scrolls meticulously stored in stone niches. Unlike the Dead Sea Scrolls found in the Qumran caves, these texts were carefully concealed, almost as if they were meant to be forgotten by time.

Leo, who had been investigating the far end of the chamber, called out, "I think I've found something. It's another set of tunnels, but these seem to lead upwards, back towards the surface."

The group gathered around the entrance to the new tunnel, the air thick with anticipation. As they moved cautiously forward, the tunnel began to narrow, forcing them to walk single file. The passage gradually inclined, and they could feel the air growing warmer, indicating that they were getting closer to the surface.

Suddenly, the tunnel opened up into a small, dimly lit chamber. In the centre of the room stood a large stone table, its surface covered in ancient tools and parchment. The walls were adorned with faded frescoes, depicting scenes of both battle and prayer. It was clear that this chamber had served as a meeting place, a secret council room where the Sicarii and Seraphimites had come together.

"This must have been where they planned," Leo said, his voice reverent. "Where they decided how to protect what was most important to them."

Petrucia, still holding the scroll she had found, began to translate its contents aloud. "It speaks of a covenant, an agreement between the two groups. The Sicarii would protect the Seraphimites and their writings, while the Seraphimites would preserve the knowledge and beliefs that the Sicarii fought to defend. They believed that their collaboration was sanctioned by Adonai, that it was a sacred duty."

The group stood in silence, absorbing the weight of this discovery. The Sicarii and the Seraphimites, though fundamentally different in their approaches, had found a way to come together in the face of overwhelming odds. They had shared a vision, a commitment to preserving their faith and heritage, even if it meant making alliances that would have been unthinkable in less dire times.

As they prepared to leave the chamber, Papa turned to the group, his eyes shining with pride and determination. "This is more than just a historical footnote. It's a testament to the power of unity in the face of destruction. The Sicarii and Seraphimites remind us that, even in the most challenging times, we can find common ground if the cause is righteous."

The group nodded in agreement, a new sense of purpose filling them. They had uncovered not just a hidden city, but a hidden truth about the resilience and unity of the human spirit. As they retraced their steps back through the tunnels, they knew that their journey was far from over. They had only scratched the surface of the secrets that these ancient walls held, and they were determined to uncover them all.

Davvie, walking next to Addie, gave her a sideways glance, his earlier uncertainty now replaced with a burgeoning excitement. "You know, Addie, maybe this is exactly where we're supposed to be. Figuring this out, uncovering these stories—it's more than just an adventure. It's a chance to understand something truly extraordinary."

Addie smiled back at him, a sense of shared purpose shining in her eyes. "You're right, Davvie. We're here for a reason. Let's see where this journey takes us."

And with that, the group moved forward, deeper into the unknown, united in their quest for truth and discovery.

6

The Sicarii's Role

The Sicarii played a pivotal role in the preservation of invaluable treasures during a time of intense conflict. As a group of Jewish zealots vehemently opposed to Roman rule, they were determined to protect their cultural and religious heritage from being eradicated. As the Roman forces laid siege to various strongholds, including Masada, the Sicarii took refuge in the elaborate tunnels beneath the Judean Mountains. These tunnels became sanctuaries, not only for the people but also for the sacred artifacts that defined their identity.

The Sicarii were acutely aware of the significance of these relics—sacred scrolls, ceremonial objects, and other symbols of their faith. They knew that losing these treasures to the Romans would be a devastating blow, not just materially but spiritually, as these items embodied the very essence of their culture and beliefs. To prevent this, they employed clever tactics to conceal the artifacts within the tunnels. False walls, hidden compartments, and intricate camouflage were all part of their strategy to ensure that their heritage would survive, even if they did not.

The partnership between the Sicarii and the Seraphimites, a secretive sect dedicated to preserving sacred knowledge, was born out of necessity. Together, they undertook the construction of a subterranean city beneath Qumran. This hidden city, connected by tunnels to Masada and Ein Gedi, became a clandestine repository for their most cherished treasures. The tunnels, initially designed for escape and storage, were expanded and fortified, transforming into a complex network that could house entire communities if needed.

The Sicarii's efforts to preserve these treasures were more than just acts of concealment; they were acts of defiance against the overwhelming power of the Roman Empire. Every artifact hidden away was a symbol of their resistance, a declaration that their culture and faith would not be obliterated by foreign conquest. The corridors of the underground city echoed with their resolve, where every stone and every hidden cache bore witness to their unwavering commitment to their people's survival.

Centuries later, a team of archaeologists unearthed these hidden treasures, revealing a story that had long been buried beneath the sands of time. The artifacts—scrolls, ceremonial objects, and more—told a tale of a people determined to preserve their identity at any cost. The Sicarii emerged not only as guardians of relics but as torchbearers of a cultural flame that refused to be extinguished. Their efforts were not merely a historical footnote but a testament to the indomitable spirit of a community that chose to pass on its legacy to future generations, even in the face of seemingly insurmountable challenges.

In a hidden chapter of history, a small group of Sicarii, driven by a mysterious calling, embarked on a journey that would take them far beyond the borders of Judea. Guided by whispers of a divine vision, they set out on an extraordinary mission that would eventually lead them to the remote village of Domrémy in ancient France. There, they encountered a young girl named Jeanne, who would later be known to the world as Joan of Arc. Recognizing the divine spark within her, the Sicarii saw a higher purpose in Jeanne's destiny, one that resonated deeply with their own history of resistance and defiance against tyranny.

Jeanne, a young girl with piercing eyes and an unyielding spirit, had experienced visions that transcended the boundaries of time and space. In the solitude of her village, she had heard the call of Papa, a divine calling that urged her to rise against oppression and liberate her homeland. The Sicarii, guided by their profound understanding of the divine, sensed that Jeanne was the vessel through which Papa's will would manifest. They approached her with reverence and purpose, revealing their own history and the parallels they saw in her mission. In that remote village, a sacred alliance was forged between the ancient warriors and the teenage girl chosen by the heavens.

The Sicarii, masters of guerrilla warfare and the art of resistance, took Jeanne under their wing, training her in the ways of combat. They shared the skills they had honed in the labyrinthine tunnels beneath Masada, teaching her the secrets of stealth, strategy, and the courage needed to face overwhelming odds. But their training went beyond physical combat; it was about instilling in Jeanne a deep sense of purpose and resilience. They spoke of the sacrifices their brethren had made in the name of freedom and how their struggle reverberated through the ages. To the Sicarii, Jeanne was not just a warrior; she was the embodiment of a divine plan that transcended borders and epochs.

As Jeanne embraced her training with unwavering determination, a bond formed between her and the Sicarii—a bond forged in the crucible of shared purpose and destiny. Together, they prepared for the battles that lay ahead, both on earthly battlegrounds and in the ethereal realm where Papa's will unfolded. In this extraordinary alliance between a medieval visionary and ancient warriors, the Sicarii's legacy found new meaning. Jeanne, armed not only with the physical skills imparted by her mentors but also with the spiritual strength drawn from their shared history, stood ready to embark on a journey that would alter the course of history.

As Jeanne led her armies into battle, the teachings of the Sicarii echoed in her every move. Their strategies, their courage, their unwavering faith—all were reflected in the young woman who would come to be known as the Maid of Orléans. And as she fought, the legacy of the Sicarii lived on, carried forward by the woman they had trained and the cause she had embraced. The Sicarii's role was no longer confined to the tunnels beneath Judea; it had expanded across time and space, influencing events that would shape the future of entire nations.

In the end, the Sicarii's mission was not just about preserving relics; it was about preserving the spirit of resistance, the belief that no matter how great the odds, there is always a reason to fight for what is right. Through Jeanne, the Sicarii's legacy found a new vessel, one that would carry their flame into the heart of Europe. Their influence, once limited to the hidden tunnels of Judea, now echoed across centuries, a reminder that the fight for freedom and identity is a timeless struggle. The pact they had made with Jeanne was a continuation of their ancient mission, a mission that had always been about more than just survival—it was about ensuring that the values they fought for would endure.

As Jeanne led her final charge, the spirit of the Sicarii was with her, guiding her actions and inspiring those who followed her. Their teachings had prepared her for the challenges she faced, and their legacy gave her the strength to confront her destiny. In this way, the Sicarii lived on, not just as a historical group but as a symbol of resistance and the unbreakable will of those who fight for their beliefs. The story of the Sicarii and Jeanne is a testament to the power of conviction, the enduring nature of cultural identity, and the ways in which history's threads can weave together across time and space, creating a tapestry of resistance that continues to inspire and guide future generations.

7

The Tunnel of Spirits

As the darkness settled over the ancient tunnels that snaked between Masada and Qumran, a palpable tension filled the air. Drew and Alexandria stood back-to-back in the narrow passageway, their hearts pounding in their chests. The flickering torchlight cast ominous shadows on the walls, making it difficult to distinguish between the shifting shadows and the lurking spirits. Their eyes, sharp and vigilant, scanned the dimly lit corridor, alert to any sign of movement. They were keenly aware that their journey through the tunnels was fraught with danger.

Their quest had been guided by Papa, who had communicated sacred instructions through Petrucia, their foremother who had taken on human form to aid them. Alongside them were Yeshua, Ruah, and Moshe, the active warrior angel, who moved seamlessly between heaven and earth to combat the forces of darkness. Mirabelle and Jeanne d'Arc, fierce and valiant friends, had also joined them on this perilous journey. Yet, despite their formidable allies, the tunnels were filled with an unsettling energy, as if the very air vibrated with malevolence.

But the desolate tunnels were not empty. Disembodied spirits, masquerading as Sicarii, lurked in the darkness, their evil presence sending shivers down the spines of the living. These wayward souls, once human, had succumbed to the dark side and now served the demonic forces that threatened to encroach upon the realm of Heaven. Their distorted forms, twisted by hatred and malice, were a far cry from the brave warriors they had once been. Now, they were agents of darkness, bent on destroying anyone who dared to oppose them.

Drew and Alexandria tightened their grip on their weapons, wielding scythes and daggers, ready to face the otherworldly malevolence. The tension in the air was so thick it was almost suffocating. The Sicarii spirits, draped in the ghostly forms they had worn in their mortal lives, emerged from the shadows, their eyes glowing with an unholy fervour. Their spectral weapons shimmered in the dim light, exuding a dark energy that seemed to drain the very life from the air around them.

"Stay strong, my love," Alexandria murmured, her voice trembling under the weight of their divine mission. Drew nodded, his jaw set with unwavering determination, as they prepared to confront the supernatural threat. Leo and Davvie, Claudine and Adeline were watching from a distance, their hearts filled with both fear and pride for their brave parents. The children's faces were pale, their eyes wide with a mixture of awe and terror as they witnessed their parents stand against the encroaching darkness.

Petrucia, her ethereal form radiating heavenly light, raised her hand, summoning a protective barrier of brilliance that enveloped the group. The light was warm and comforting, a stark contrast to the cold malevolence that filled the tunnel. Yeshua stood in prayer, keenly aware that he was not to participate in the battle, but to stand back and offer up petitions for these dear ones. Ruah whispered words of wisdom and guidance, her presence a calming influence amid the gathering storm. The air hummed with the power of their combined faith, creating a palpable force that pushed back against the darkness.

The first Sicarii spirit lunged at Drew with a savage snarl, wielding a wicked scythe that glinted menacingly in the torchlight. Drew met the attack head-on, the sound of clashing metal reverberating through the tunnel. Sparks flew as steel met ethereal force. The impact of their clash sent shockwaves through the air, shaking the very walls of the tunnel. Drew gritted his teeth, his muscles straining as he pushed back against the spirit's overwhelming strength. With a powerful strike, Drew disarmed the spirit, sending it reeling back into the inky depths. The spirit let out a wail of fury and pain as it dissolved into the shadows, its form unravelling into wisps of darkness.

Alexandria faced her own assailant, a Sicarii spirit brandishing a dagger with evil intent. The spirit's eyes burned with a sinister glow as it lunged at her, its movements quick and deadly. She moved with grace and precision, deftly dodging the spirit's thrusts and counterattacking with her scythe. Her movements were fluid, almost dance-like, as she twisted and turned, avoiding the spirit's attacks with an agility that belied the seriousness of the situation. With a swift, fluid motion, she knocked the dagger from the spirit's grip and delivered a decisive blow, causing it to disintegrate into the cold, desolate air. The spirit let out a final, anguished cry as it faded into nothingness, its presence erased from the tunnel.

Mirabelle and Jeanne d'Arc fought in perfect harmony, their weapons a whirlwind of deadly motion. Mirabelle's gleaming sword danced in the torchlight as she parried the attacks of two Sicarii spirits, her footwork nimble and exact. Her movements were a blur of steel and light, each strike delivered with pinpoint accuracy. Jeanne d'Arc, with her fiery determination, swung her mighty sword with unwavering resolve, cleaving through the unholy foes that surrounded her. Her strikes were powerful and decisive, each one sending a Sicarii spirit crumbling into the shadows. Together, they formed an unstoppable force, their synergy creating a deadly dance of steel and light.

Moshe soared through the darkness with celestial wings, engaging the Sicarii spirits in fierce combat. His sword of light clashed with theirs, dispelling their malevolence with each powerful stroke. The spirits recoiled from his divine presence, their forms disintegrating as his sword cut through their ethereal bodies. Moshe moved with the grace and power of a warrior who had fought countless battles, his every strike a testament to his celestial strength.

As the battle continued, the Sicarii spirits grew increasingly desperate. They swarmed the group, their numbers seemingly endless. Their once-coordinated attacks became frenzied, driven by a primal fear of the light that now threatened to consume them. But the divine radiance that enveloped Drew and Alexandria and their companions was unyielding. The light shone brighter with each passing moment, pushing back the darkness and filling the tunnel with a warmth that the spirits could not withstand. The tide of the battle began to turn in their favour as the spirits' attacks grew weaker and more disorganized.

Petrucia, her eyes blazing with heavenly radiance, summoned a celestial choir, their harmonious voices filling the tunnel with a transcendent melody. The hauntingly beautiful music swelled, washing over the Sicarii spirits like a tidal wave, disorienting them and sapping their strength. The spirits clutched at their heads, their faces contorted in agony as the music overwhelmed their senses. They staggered and stumbled, their once-menacing forms now reduced to pitiful shadows of their former selves.

Yeshua's presence intensified, and the Sicarii spirits, unable to bear the radiant love he emanated, faltered and withered. Some dropped to their knees, tears streaming down their spectral faces as they were overwhelmed by the profound grace of his compassion. They reached out, as if seeking redemption, but their time had passed. The light enveloped them, dissolving their forms into the ether, leaving nothing but a sense of peace in their wake.

Drew and Alexandria, invigorated by the divine forces that encircled them, pressed forward with renewed resolve. They fought with a unity that left the Sicarii spirits with no avenue of escape. Their movements were perfectly synchronized, each strike and parry flowing seamlessly into the next. One by one, the spirits were vanquished, their twisted forms dissipating into the abyss. The tunnel echoed with the sounds of their final cries as they were banished from the mortal realm.

Finally, the tunnel fell silent, save for the waning echoes of the celestial choir. The battle had been won, and the evil spirits that had threatened to breach the realm of Heaven had been banished. Drew and Alexandria, their bodies adorned with sweat and grime, stood victorious, their weapons at the ready. The air was thick with the aftermath of the battle, the scent of ozone lingering in the tunnel.

Petrucia, her heavenly form radiant with light, smiled at them. "You have confronted the darkness and emerged triumphant," she said, her voice filled with pride and gratitude. The light around her shimmered, casting a warm glow over the group.

Yeshua drew near, his eyes brimming with love and warmth. "Your faith and love have brought us victory this day," he said, placing a hand on Drew and Alexandria's shoulders. His touch was gentle, yet it carried the weight of divine approval.

Ruah encircled them with her comforting presence. "You are true champions of the light," she whispered, her voice akin to a gentle zephyr. The air around them seemed to hum with a soft, soothing energy, as if the very fabric of the tunnel had been infused with peace.

Mirabelle and Jeanne d'Arc, their swords still gleaming, embraced Drew and Alexandria. "We couldn't have done it without you," Mirabelle said with a smile, her eyes brimming with admiration. Jeanne nodded in agreement, her expression one of deep respect.

The once ominous tunnel, now bathed in a soft, glorious radiance, had been transformed. The battle had been arduous, but the love and unity of the group had emerged triumphant, and the forces of Heaven had prevailed. The air was filled with a sense of victory and relief, the oppressive darkness replaced by a gentle light.

As they moved through the tunnel and back into the open expanse of the desert, they recognized that their mission was far from over. The battle they had just fought was only one step in their journey, and they knew they would face many more trials before their journey was complete. The group emerged from the tunnel, their eyes adjusting to the open sky above. The stars twinkled in the night, a reminder of the celestial forces that had aided them in their battle.

After the battle had concluded, the dust of the skirmish began to settle, and Claudine, Leo, Adeline, and Davvie stood at the tunnel's entrance, their eyes wide with a mixture of astonishment and admiration. They beheld their parents, Alexandria and Drew, who moments ago had wielded swords and fought with an incredible skill that seemed incongruent with the familiar image of Eema and Abba. The siblings were caught in a moment of profound surprise, their expressions mirroring the awe that lingered in the air.

Never before had they witnessed their parents engaged in battle, let alone brandishing weapons with such finesse. It was a spectacle that shattered the routine of domesticity and revealed a hidden aspect of their family's reality. The questions naturally bubbled to the surface, and Adeline, with a mix of amazement and curiosity, voiced what all of them were thinking.

"Where did you learn to fight like that?" she asked, her gaze shifting between her parents. The air was filled with a palpable sense of inquiry, the siblings eager to unravel the mystery behind this newfound facet of their parents' lives.

In response, Alex and Drew exchanged knowing smiles, a shared acknowledgment of a tale waiting to be unveiled. Their eyes drifted towards Jeanne d'Arc, their friend and comrade in arms, who stood nearby with a serene yet authoritative presence. The connection between the trio held a depth that surpassed mere camaraderie; it was a bond forged in the crucible of battles against otherworldly adversaries.

"It's thanks to Jeanne," Alexandria began, her voice carrying both gratitude and respect. "She trained with the Sicarii in her day and has been our guiding force in honing our skills for battles such as these."

Drew added, "Jeanne's knowledge and experiences have been invaluable to us. She has imparted the wisdom of her own battles against the Sicarii and has been instrumental in guiding us through our training."

Jeanne, humbly acknowledging the acknowledgment, nodded with a sense of quiet satisfaction. She had transitioned from the historical pages into the present, carrying with her not only the echoes of her own battles but the determination to pass on her acquired skills to the next generation of warriors.

As the siblings absorbed this revelation, they began to understand that their parents had embarked on a unique journey, guided by the wisdom of a legendary figure. They realized that the battles fought by their parents were not just about survival; they were about protecting a legacy that transcended time and space.

The air was charged with a newfound respect for the complexity of their family's legacy, where everyday roles intertwined with a responsibility to stand against unearthly forces. This realization brought them closer together, their bond strengthened by the knowledge that they were part of something far greater than they had ever imagined.

As the family and their companions stood together in the aftermath of the battle, they knew that their journey was far from over. The road ahead would be filled with challenges, but they would face them as a united front, bolstered by the love and faith that had carried them through this trial. The Sicarii, Jeanne, and their heavenly allies had shown them the way, and they were ready to continue the fight, whatever the future might hold.

And so, with renewed determination and the strength of their shared purpose, they set out once more into the night, their hearts alight with the knowledge that they had faced the darkness and emerged victorious. The tunnel of spirits, once a place of dread, had become a symbol of their triumph—a testament to the power of love, faith, and unity in the face of overwhelming odds.

8

The Solo Quest

Amidst the celebrations of their newfound treasure, the air buzzed with excitement and curiosity. The family and celestial companions gathered around, marveling at the ancient artifact they had uncovered. Laughter and conversation filled the site, but Adeline felt a gentle nudge on her shoulder. She turned to see Papa, his eyes filled with a knowing and tender light.

"Adeline, come walk with me, beloved daughter," Papa spoke, his voice gentle yet purposeful.

Curiosity piqued, Adeline nodded and followed him a short distance away. The moonlight bathed the Qumran site in a silvery glow, and the noise of the celebration faded into the background. Papa stopped, his expression more serious.

"Adeline," he began, "there is something important we need to discuss. While your family is here to support this quest, there is another task that requires your unique abilities."

Adeline's heart quickened. "Another task?" she whispered.

Papa nodded. "Yes, a solo journey that only you can undertake."

Adeline's mind raced, but before she could speak, Papa continued. "Do you remember the dream you had about Te Ata Whetu?"

A shiver ran down her spine. The dream had been vivid and powerful. "Yes, I remember," she whispered.

Papa's eyes softened. "Te Ata Whetu, your guardian angel, showed you glimpses of your heritage and a greater purpose. That vision was no mere dream; it was a divine call to action."

Adeline steadied her nerves. "What must I do?"

"You must meet Te Ata Whetu at the cliffs of the Sea of Salt," Papa explained. "She will reveal the next steps of your journey, helping you understand your spiritual heritage and the path ahead."

Adeline felt a mixture of excitement and trepidation. "But why me, Papa? Why not someone more experienced?"

Papa smiled gently, radiating love and assurance. "Your faith, curiosity, and ability to see beyond the ordinary make you the perfect person for this task. And remember, I am with you always."

The weight of responsibility settled on her, but so did a profound sense of purpose. "What do I need to do?" she asked, more determined.

"You will travel to the cliffs of the Sea of Salt at dawn. Trust in Me and in the guidance of Te Ata Whetu."

Adeline nodded, her resolve growing. "I'll do it."

Papa placed a comforting hand on her shoulder. "Now, go back and enjoy this moment with your family. You will leave at first light."

As they walked back to the group, Adeline's thoughts were already on the journey ahead. It would be challenging, but she could not ignore this calling.

Later that night, as the family gathered around the campfire, Adeline sat quietly, absorbing the warmth and love that surrounded her. She watched her mother, Alexandria, and her siblings, feeling a mixture of joy and bittersweet anticipation. Her departure would concern them, but this was a journey she had to take alone.

The night passed with shared laughter and memories. Adeline's heart swelled with gratitude, knowing that her family would be with her in spirit, even though the path ahead was hers to walk. As they told stories under the flickering campfire light, Adeline glanced around at her loved ones—her mother, father, siblings, and companions—each one supporting her in their own way. She cherished these final moments with them, the warmth of their love strengthening her resolve.

As dawn approached, Adeline quietly packed her essentials and slipped away from the camp. The path to the Sea of Salt stretched before her, bathed in the soft light of the rising sun. She took a deep breath, feeling Papa's presence and Te Ata Whetu's guidance.

With one last look at the sleeping camp, Adeline set off. The cool air brushed her skin, and the sky, streaked with pink and gold, seemed to welcome her. Her footsteps echoed in the stillness of the morning as she neared the cliffs, each step filled with anticipation and purpose.

As she approached the cliffs, the Sea of Salt glimmering in the distance, the memory of her dream returned with clarity. Te Ata Whetu had appeared to her, revealing her connection to ancient cultures—Maori, Viking, and Celtic—and showing her a divine purpose that stretched beyond the ordinary.

Reaching the cliffs, Adeline saw a figure standing at the edge, silhouetted against the rising sun. It was Te Ata Whetu, draped in a korowai. Her angelic guide's presence filled Adeline with peace.

"Te Ata Whetu," Adeline called out, her voice steady despite the weight of the moment.

Te Ata Whetu turned, her eyes filled with ancient wisdom and love. "Welcome, Adeline. You have come far. Now we begin the next part of your journey."

Adeline stood at the edge of the cliffs, the vast sea before her. "What must I do?" she asked, her voice tinged with both awe and trepidation.

Te Ata Whetu smiled. "Listen to the still, small voice of Adonai, to Ruah the Holy Spirit, and to the calling of your heart."

Adeline's heart raced as she stepped closer to the cliff's edge. The sound of crashing waves below filled her ears, the wind pulling at her hair. The sea stretched out before her like an invitation.

Te Ata Whetu gestured to the water. "The answers you seek are not above, but in the depths below. Dive into the heart of creation, and you will find the truth."

Adeline stared at the churning waters, dread rising in her chest. Diving into the cold, dark sea seemed terrifying, but she knew this was her path.

With a deep breath, she nodded to Te Ata Whetu. "I understand."

Te Ata Whetu placed a reassuring hand on her shoulder. "Trust in Yeshua with all your heart. Papa is with you always."

With a final glance at her angelic guide, Adeline stepped off the cliff and plunged into the sea below. The cold water shocked her senses, but she pressed on, swimming deeper into the abyss. Darkness enveloped her, but even here, she felt Papa's nearness.

As she swam further, the presence of Ruah led her, guiding her deeper. The truth she sought was not far now. At last, she reached the bottom, the sea floor stretching out before her. There, in the sand, a small stone glimmered. Adeline reached out and grasped it, warmth spreading through her as Ruah's voice filled her mind.

The journey back to the surface was swift, as if the sea itself carried her upward. Gasping for air, she broke through the surface and swam to shore. Te Ata Whetu was waiting for her, eyes filled with pride.

"You have done well, Adeline. The stone is a key—a connection to your spiritual heritage. In time, its purpose will be revealed."

Adeline looked at the stone in her hand, its carvings glowing faintly. She felt a deep sense of purpose, knowing this was more than just an artifact—it was a guide to her destiny.

That night, as the family gathered around the campfire once more, Adeline felt a deep sense of peace. She shared with them the details of her journey, the stone she had found, and the divine calling she felt deep within her soul. Her family listened with awe, their faces a mixture of pride and support. Though her next step would take her away from them, she knew their prayers would follow her every step of the way.

The flames of the campfire flickered, casting warm light on the faces of those gathered around. Adeline cherished these final moments, surrounded by the love and encouragement of her family. She looked around at each of them—her mother and father, her siblings, and celestial companions—and felt an overwhelming sense of gratitude.

But as the night wore on and the family began to drift off to sleep, Adeline remained awake, her thoughts focused on the journey ahead. The stone pulsed faintly in her hand, its warmth comforting her. She stared into the darkness, feeling a strange sense of anticipation in the stillness of the night.

Just as the first light of dawn began to creep over the horizon, a chill ran down her spine. The warmth of the stone faded, replaced by an eerie cold. Her breath caught as she looked up.

Far beyond the camp, silhouetted against the distant horizon, stood a figure. Tall and foreboding, the shadow seemed to pulse with a darkness that sent shivers through her. It was distant, unmoving, yet she knew—he was watching.

Adeline's pulse quickened. She didn't need to know who he was to sense the danger. Whoever—or whatever—it was, the figure wasn't a friend.

She clutched the stone tighter. This was only the beginning.

9

Adeline's Heartcry

Adeline stood on the precipice of her faith, gazing into the depths of her church history. The scars of disappointment and pain marked a journey that had left her questioning the very foundations of her beliefs. The sanctuary, once a haven of solace, now echoed with the haunting memories of broken trust and shattered ideals.

Having been raised in a single-parent family, Adeline bore the weight of additional burdens within the church community. The whispers of judgment and the cold glances, already prevalent due to the flaws of the human condition, intensified when her family structure deviated from the perceived norm. The subtle marginalization and ostracism she experienced cut deep, creating wounds that intertwined with the broader narrative of her struggles with faith.

The church, an institution meant to embody love and compassion, had, for Adeline, become a battlefield of contradictions.

The wounds ran deep, inflicted not only by external judgment but also by the internal struggle to reconcile her convictions with the flawed humanity she witnessed within those sacred walls.

She had seen the hypocrisy, the power struggles, and the selective compassion that seemed to betray the very essence of the teachings she held dear. The echoes of whispered gossip, the judgmental glances, and the painful exclusion had etched themselves onto her spirit, creating a chasm between the faith she desired and the reality she experienced.

Adeline grappled not only with the dichotomy of a God who preached love and acceptance but also with the harsh reality that her family structure had become a source of exclusion within the church. The pain of feeling doubly marginalized, both for her faith and her family circumstances, left her heart wounded and her faith fragile.

In the solitude of her contemplation, Adeline sought answers. She longed for a connection between her faith, her family history, and her church experience—a bridge to span the gap between the divine and the flawed human vessels through which it was conveyed. Yet, the pain lingered, and the questions remained unanswered.

The church's teachings, once a source of guidance, now felt like a distant echo. Adeline grappled with the inconsistencies in the Bible, the historical manipulations, and the omissions that cast shadows of doubt on the authenticity of the sacred text. The council of Nicaea and the removal of certain books left her questioning the purity of the message she had held onto for so long.

Yet, despite the tumult within her, Adeline clung to a flicker of belief. It was a small ember, fueled by the undeniable presence of a divine force she felt in moments of solitude and contemplation. The struggle to reconcile her faith with the flawed nature of humans persisted, but she dared to hope that, in time, the wounds would heal, and a more profound understanding would emerge.

As Adeline stood at the crossroads of faith and disillusionment, she yearned for a revelation—a divine whisper that would guide her through the labyrinth of doubts and lead her to a place of peace and acceptance. The journey was not only about reclaiming her faith but also about finding a place within her spiritual community that embraced the uniqueness of herself and her family story.

***

Adeline, pondering the complexities of the Bible's evolution, turned to Te Ata Whetu with a furrowed brow. "Te Ata Whetu," she began, "I find myself grappling with the Bible and its many versions throughout history. The translations, the alterations that have changed women's names to masculine names, and the chapters, words, and definitions that have been omitted or modified. How can I fully entrust my belief in this 'book' when it has undergone such profound transformation over the millennia, regardless of the intentions, good or bad, of those involved?"

Te Ata Whetu listened with empathy, understanding the weight of Adeline's concerns. "Adeline," she said gently, "the Bible, like all sacred texts, has been subject to interpretation and adaptation throughout history. While some changes were made with good intentions, others were influenced by human fallibility and political motives. However, the essence of the message remains unchanged."

She continued, "It is important to remember that the Bible, despite its seeming contradictions, contains timeless truths and teachings that transcend the limitations of language and culture. The key is to approach the Bible with discernment and an open heart, seeking the guidance of Ruah to illuminate its meaning for you. Also remember, sweet child, Papa is the one who breathed upon each individual who wrote their section. This document originated in his heart."

Adeline nodded, a sense of peace settling over her. "Thank you, Te Ata Whetu," she said, "for helping me navigate these complexities. I will strive to approach the Bible with discernment and an open heart, trusting in the guidance of Ruah."

Suddenly Papa appeared in their midst. He grinned mischievously, his presence a source of comfort and assurance for Adeline. Suddenly, he reached out and mussed up her hair, causing her to laugh and playfully swat at his hand.

"Hey, none of that!" Adeline protested, trying to smooth down her unruly locks.

"Ah, but you look so much more like a warrior with your hair askew!" Papa chuckled, twirling her around before they continued their journey of faith. Together, they navigated the complexities of scripture with wisdom, grace, and a touch of playful banter. Te Ata Whetu smiled and giggled at the two at play.

10

The Longing

Adeline's longing for a genuine connection with Yeshua echoed within the depths of her soul. The stories of her parents and sister, their palpable experiences with the divine, left her with a yearning to unravel the mysteries that had eluded her thus far. She watched as their faces lit up with a divine radiance, and their hearts seemed to dance with the rhythm of a divine melody.

Her quest to understand the true essence of Yeshua became a pilgrimage of the heart, a journey to untangle the threads of doubt and scepticism that had woven themselves into the fabric of her faith. She sought not just the teachings found in ancient texts but a living, breathing relationship with the divine, a connection that transcended the confines of earthly interpretations.

In the quiet moments of solitude, Adeline found herself whispering prayers, seeking the presence of Yeshua to manifest in her life as it had for her family. She craved the experiences that would bridge the gap between the intellectual understanding of her faith and the intimate, soul-stirring encounters she witnessed in those she loved.

The pain of past church wounds and the complexities of her family history served as barriers to the divine communion she sought. Yet, Adeline pressed on, determined to peel back the layers of doubt and disappointment, and to stand before Yeshua with an open heart and unburdened spirit.

She delved into the scriptures, not merely as a text but as a portal to the living Yeshua. The stories of compassion, healing, and love took on new meaning as she yearned to experience those transformative moments firsthand. Adeline immersed herself in prayer, scripture reading, and contemplation, inviting Yeshua into the very fabric of her being.

The journey was not without its challenges. The old scars and wounds often cast shadows on her path. Yet, Adeline's persistence became a testament to her unwavering faith and her unyielding desire for a personal relationship with the divine.

As she stood on the clifftop, overlooking her history with Te Ata Whetu, Adeline extended an invitation to Yeshua. With arms outstretched and heart laid bare, she whispered, "Reveal yourself to me, not as tradition dictates, but as the living, breathing essence of love and truth. Let me walk with you as my family has, and let your presence be the guiding light through the wondering halls of my faith."

Having just poured out her heart, inviting Yeshua to make himself known, to bridge the gap between her and the divine. Little did she know that her prayer had been heard, and a revelation was about to unfold.

In the quiet aftermath of her heartfelt plea, Adeline sensed a presence. It started as a soft warmth, an invisible embrace that encircled her, and then, slowly but unmistakably, a figure materialized before her. Yeshua stood there, not in the distant echoes of ancient tales, but in the vivid reality of the present moment.

Adeline's surprise and relief mingled as tears welled in her eyes. His presence was tangible, a manifestation that transcended the boundaries of time and doubt. The divine figure before her emanated a serene glow, and his eyes held a depth of compassion that spoke to the very core of her being.

"Why now?" Adeline's voice trembled as she spoke. "I sought you for so long, for years, and it seemed my prayers fell on deaf ears. I even chose to walk a path without you, to put it all on the shelf and forge a new life. Why reveal yourself to me now?"

Yeshua's response was not audible but resonated within her heart. It was a whisper of understanding, a gentle reassurance that time and divine timing were intricately woven into the fabric of her spiritual journey. The moments of seeking and the apparent silence were not a neglectful absence but a preparation for a revelation beyond her expectations.

As Adeline questioned, Yeshua's gaze held a profound kindness. The answers unfolded not in a torrent but as a gradual unveiling. His divine figure spoke through the language of the heart, addressing her years of longing, her moments of desperation, and the silent anguish she carried.

"You sought me with a genuine heart, Adeline. The journey was not in vain, for even in the moments you felt abandoned, I was there, weaving the tapestry of your faith. The timing of revelation is as important as the revelation itself. Sometimes, the depth of connection requires a journey through the valleys of doubt and the shadows of seeking."

Adeline, now enveloped in the radiance of Yeshua's presence, felt a peace that transcended understanding. The weight of her questions had not disappeared entirely, but in that moment, she realized that some answers were beyond words. Yeshua's presence was the response, a tangible affirmation of a connection that had always been, even when she felt it was absent.

With a gentle smile, Yeshua extended his hand to Adeline, inviting her to walk alongside him in the unfolding chapters of her life. The clifftop breeze carried a whispered assurance—the divine, ever-present, ever-loving, had revealed itself in a way that surpassed the limitations of human understanding.

Yeshua's voice, like a melody echoing through the mountains, spoke to Adeline's soul. "Adeline, my beloved, I have heard every prayer, felt every longing, and witnessed every tear. Your journey has been a testament to your genuine seeking, and it has not gone unnoticed."

He gestured towards the panoramic view from the cliffs, where the world stretched out below them. "Just as you stand here, overlooking the vast expanse of your history, I've been with you in every step of your journey. In moments of joy and despair, in times of seeking and times of surrender, I have walked beside you."

Adeline, still absorbing the presence of Yeshua, felt a mixture of emotions—gratitude, awe, and a lingering ache from the years of longing. "Why did it take so long?" she asked again, her voice a fragile whisper in the grandeur of the moment.

Yeshua's eyes, filled with compassion, met hers. "Time, in the realm of the divine, is not measured as it is on Earth. The unfolding of revelation aligns with the rhythm of your soul's growth. The tapestry of your faith is intricately woven, and each thread, whether perceived as light or shadow, contributes to the masterpiece of your spiritual journey."

He continued, "There is no condemnation for the moments you chose to walk a path without me. I understand the weariness and the need for respite. The shelf you placed your faith upon was not a separation; it was a sacred pause, a space for you to breathe and reassess."

Adeline, sensing a profound truth in his words, felt the weight of guilt lifting. Yeshua's presence brought not only answers but a gentle release from the burdens she had carried for so long.

"In the seeking, you have found," Yeshua said, his voice like a gentle breeze that caressed her soul. "And in the moments of silence, I have been present. Your faith, Adeline, is not defined by the absence of challenges or unanswered questions; it is a living, breathing expression of your heart's connection to us, the divine."

As they walked together upon the clifftop, Yeshua shared stories—stories of love, forgiveness, and the unending grace that flowed from the divine source. Each narrative resonated with Adeline's own journey, weaving a tapestry that connected the ancient teachings with the intimate moments of her life.

The jagged cliffs, once a symbol of isolation, became a sacred space where Adeline's faith was reborn. Yeshua walked with her, not just in the extraordinary moments but in the ordinary, the mundane, and the intricacies of her daily existence.

The revelation was not a conclusion but a continuation—a journey where faith, now intimately connected with experience, would unfold like the pages of a divine storybook. As Adeline and Yeshua descended from the cliffs, a newfound sense of peace and purpose illuminated their path. The whispers of the sacred surrounded them, and the divine presence once sought in desperation, had become a constant companion in the symphony of Adeline's life.

Adeline's journey toward the true Yeshua was a pilgrimage of the soul, a quest for an authentic encounter that transcended doctrine and touched the very core of her being. And in that sacred pursuit, she discovered that sometimes, the most profound revelations come not in grand displays but in the quiet whispers of the heart.

11

The Parables of Yeshua

"The story of the lost sheep, are you familiar with that, Adeline?"

"Yes, of course. But I'd love to hear it from your perspective, here and now," Adeline replied, her curiosity piqued as she walked beside Yeshua through the ancient fortress. The air was thick with the weight of history, and every step seemed to echo with the stories of the past.

Yeshua smiled warmly, a gentle light shining in his eyes. "In this story," he began, "the shepherd's love for each individual sheep is a reflection of Papa's unwavering love for each of His children. Your journey, Adeline, is a pursuit of that love, and in every step, Papa seeks to bring you back into the embrace of His grace."

Adeline nodded, urging him to continue, eager to hear the timeless parable through his divine lens.

As Yeshua continued to share the parable of the Lost Sheep, the ancient stones of the fortress seemed to resonate with the power of the story. It was as if the walls themselves were leaning in to listen, absorbing the profound truths being spoken.

"A shepherd had a flock of a hundred sheep," Yeshua began, his voice carrying a warmth that matched the gentle breeze that brushed through the fortress. "Each sheep was precious to him, known intimately by name. One day, as the sun dipped below the horizon, the shepherd realized that one sheep was missing. Without hesitation, he left the safety of the ninety-nine and ventured into the wilderness to find the one that had strayed."

Adeline listened intently, her eyes fixed on Yeshua as he painted the scene with his words. She could almost see the shepherd, anxious and determined, setting out into the vast, dark wilderness to find the lost sheep.

"In the darkness, with only the light of the moon as his guide, the shepherd sought the lost sheep tirelessly," Yeshua continued, his voice soft yet filled with conviction. "He navigated treacherous terrain, calling out its name with a longing in his heart. And finally, in the stillness of the night, he heard a faint bleat—a cry for rescue."

A soft smile played on Yeshua's lips, mirroring the shepherd's joy in the parable. "The shepherd's love for that one lost sheep was immeasurable. The ninety-nine were secure, yet his heart was incomplete without the one that had wandered. He cradled the sheep in his arms, rejoicing not just because it was found, but because the unity of the flock was restored."

Yeshua paused, allowing the significance of the story to settle. The air around them seemed to grow still as if the fortress itself were holding its breath in reverence for the message being conveyed.

"Adeline, you are that precious sheep," Yeshua continued, his voice gentle but firm. "Your journey, with its twists and turns, has not escaped the watchful eye of Papa. The seeker of lost souls traverses the wilderness of your experiences, calling your name with a love that never wavers."

Adeline's eyes glistened with a mixture of gratitude and understanding. The parable resonated deeply within her, touching on the profound truths she had been seeking. In the shepherd's relentless pursuit, she saw a reflection of her own life—the moments of wandering, the times when she had felt lost and alone, and the ever-present love of Papa that sought to bring her back into the fold.

"Papa, as the divine," Yeshua emphasized, "is not content with the safety of the majority. The depth of love reaches into the shadows, into the places where souls feel lost and disconnected. In every step you take, in every moment you question, the divine seeks to bring you back into the fold, into the completeness of His embrace."

As the parable unfolded, the fortress seemed to exhale a collective sigh—a sigh of reassurance that in the vastness of the spiritual landscape, no soul was too far or too lost to be found by the divine shepherd's unwavering love. The stones beneath their feet seemed to hum with the echoes of the story, each one bearing silent witness to the profound truth being shared.

Yeshua's gaze softened as he watched Adeline absorb the lessons of the parable. He could see the wheels of understanding turning in her mind, and he knew that the message had reached the deepest parts of her heart.

"Let's take the story of the Prodigal Son, one which I know you're all too familiar with!" Yeshua smiled in jest, to which Adeline nodded her head and giggled.

"This story," he said, his voice taking on a more serious tone, "reflects the boundless compassion of the divine. No matter how far you've strayed or how long you've wandered, Papa's love remains constant, waiting to embrace you upon your return."

Yeshua's words hung in the air, rich with meaning as he began to share the parable of the Prodigal Son, a timeless narrative that had resonated through the ages, touching countless hearts with its message of redemption and unconditional love.

"There once was a man with two sons," Yeshua began, his words weaving a tale of family, redemption, and the unwavering love of a father. "The younger son, restless and eager for independence, approached his father and asked for his share of the inheritance."

Adeline closed her eyes for a moment, imagining the scene as Yeshua described it—a father, reluctantly dividing his wealth, and a son, filled with dreams of freedom and adventure, setting off into the world.

"The younger son set off into the world, embracing the allure of freedom and indulging in every pleasure life had to offer. However, as the days turned into nights, and the seasons changed, so did the fortune of the young man. The wealth he had squandered was now gone, and he found himself in a distant land, destitute and longing for the security he had left behind."

Yeshua's eyes held a deep compassion as he continued, and Adeline could feel the weight of the son's choices, the highs of recklessness, and the inevitable lows of humility.

"In his desperation, the prodigal son decided to return home. He rehearsed the words he would say to his father, willing to be a servant in his household rather than a wayward son."

Adeline felt the weight of the son's journey—the highs of recklessness and the lows of humility—echoing the peaks and valleys of her own life. She could almost hear the son's voice, trembling with fear and regret, as he prepared to return to the father he had wronged.

"And as the son approached his father's house, a surprising turn of events unfolded. The father, who had been watching and waiting, saw his prodigal son from a distance. Overwhelmed with compassion, he ran to meet him, embraced him, and welcomed him back with open arms."

Yeshua paused, allowing the significance of the moment to settle in Adeline's heart. The joy of the father's embrace, the relief of the son's return—it was all so vivid, so real, as if she could feel the warmth of that embrace herself.

"The father didn't scold or chastise," Yeshua continued. "Instead, he threw a celebration, rejoicing in the return of his lost son. He said, 'For this son of mine was dead and is alive again; he was lost and is found.' The household celebrated not just the return of a wayward child but the restoration of a broken relationship."

Adeline's heart stirred with emotion. The prodigal son's journey mirrored her own struggles with faith, the moments of seeking, and the humbling realization that the divine's love surpassed the confines of her understanding. She thought of the times she had turned away from Papa, seeking fulfilment in the world, only to find herself longing for the safety and love of His embrace.

"The Prodigal Son," Yeshua explained, "is a story of redemption, a testament to the boundless mercy and forgiveness of Papa. No matter how far one may stray, the door to Papa's love is always open. Your journey, Adeline, is not defined by the moments you've walked away but by the embrace waiting for you upon your return."

As Yeshua concluded the parable, the ancient fortress seemed to resonate with the profound truth—Papa's love, like the father's, was a beacon of hope, ready to illuminate the path of return for every seeking soul. Adeline felt the fortress itself was bearing witness to the story, the stones whispering of the countless souls who had found their way back to the Father's embrace.

Yeshua's gaze turned to the landscape around them, and he began to share the parable of the Mustard Seed, a tale of profound simplicity and transformative growth.

"Consider the tiny mustard seed," Yeshua began, holding one between his fingers, the small grain almost disappearing in his hand. "It starts as one of the smallest seeds, seemingly insignificant in the grand tapestry of creation. Yet, when planted and nurtured, it grows into a mighty tree, providing shelter for the birds of the air."

Adeline's eyes fixed on the mustard seed, and her imagination painted a vivid picture of a seed that defied its modest beginnings. She could see it in her mind's eye—a tiny seed bursting forth from the soil, growing stronger each day until it became a towering tree, its branches offering refuge and life.

"In this small seed," Yeshua continued, "there lies the potential for exponential growth. Your faith, Adeline, is akin to this mustard seed. It may seem inconspicuous at times, but within it resides the power to blossom into something magnificent."

He gestured towards the expanse of the mountainside, where wildflowers adorned the slopes. "Your faith, no matter how small it may appear, has the capacity to take root and flourish, becoming a source of shelter and nourishment for others. It's not about the size of your faith but the sincerity with which it is planted and cultivated."

As Yeshua spoke, Adeline felt a sense of encouragement and validation. Her journey, marked by doubts and questions, was likened to the growth of the mustard seed—an intimate process that unfolded gradually, yet held the promise of profound transformation.

"Our Papa," Yeshua continued, "values the authenticity of your faith. Like the mustard seed, it's not the grandeur of your convictions that matters, but the sincerity with which you hold them. Your smallest acts of belief, when nurtured with care and intention, can yield a harvest that far exceeds your expectations."

Adeline, captivated by the symbolism of the mustard seed, found solace in the idea that her faith, though at times seemingly small and fragile, could be a force for positive change and growth.

"May you plant your faith with hope and tenderness," Yeshua concluded. "And in its growth, may you find the strength to shelter others, just as the mustard tree provides a haven for the birds seeking refuge."

As they continued their walk through the ancient fortress, the mustard seed became a symbol not only of faith but of the potential within every seeking soul—a potential to grow, to provide shelter, and to contribute to the flourishing of the spiritual landscape.

Yeshua's gaze shifted, and his expression grew more serious as he recounted the encounter with a Samaritan woman at a well, emphasizing the transformative power of living water. "The well represents the thirst of the soul," he explained. "Just as I offered living water to the woman, the divine offers the same to you. It is a source of eternal nourishment, quenching the deepest longings of your heart."

Yeshua's voice carried a deep sense of reverence as he began to share the parable of the Samaritan Woman at the Well, a story of profound encounter and spiritual transformation.

"In the town of Sychar," Yeshua began, "there was a well known as Jacob's well. One day, a Samaritan woman approached the well to draw water, and I, weary from the journey, sat there, waiting."

Adeline's imagination painted the scene—a dusty path, the ancient well, and the Samaritan woman, unaware of the extraordinary encounter that awaited her.

"The woman was surprised when I asked her for a drink, for Jews and Samaritans held no dealings. In our conversation, I spoke not only of physical water but of living water—the kind that, once received, would become a wellspring within her, flowing to eternal life."

Yeshua's eyes, filled with compassion, mirrored the transformative nature of the encounter at the well.

"As our conversation unfolded, I revealed to her the depth of her own life—the choices, the struggles, and the longing for something more. In that vulnerable exchange, the Samaritan woman's heart began to open, and she recognized that I offered not just words but a spiritual revelation that quenched a thirst deeper than any well could satisfy."

Adeline felt the weight of the Samaritan woman's journey—the layers of her life exposed and yet met with compassion and understanding.

"The Samaritan woman," Yeshua continued, "left her water jar at the well and ran to the town, proclaiming the encounter that had changed her life. The well became a symbol not just of physical sustenance but of a spiritual awakening—a place where the ordinary transformed into the extraordinary."

As Adeline absorbed the essence of the parable, Yeshua connected the story to the broader themes of her own spiritual journey.

"Adeline, like the Samaritan woman, you carry your own well of experiences and longings. Your encounters with the divine are not confined to the mundane routine of daily life but can be transformative, like the encounter at Jacob's well. The living water I offer is not bound by tradition or circumstance—it flows to quench the deepest thirst of your soul."

He paused, allowing the significance of the Samaritan woman's story to resonate.

"In your seeking, may you discover the living water within you—a source of eternal nourishment that transcends the temporal challenges and quenches the spiritual thirst that resides in the depths of your being."

As they continued their journey through the fortress, the story of the Samaritan Woman at the Well became a timeless reminder that every encounter with the divine had the potential to be a wellspring of transformation, offering a deeper understanding of oneself and the boundless grace that awaited each seeking soul.

Yeshua's steps slowed as he shared the story of providing bread to the hungry multitude, his voice gentle yet filled with the authority of one who had fed both bodies and souls. "I am the bread of life," Yeshua said, his words resonating deeply within Adeline's heart. "Just as physical bread sustains the body, the divine presence nourishes the spirit. Your hunger for meaning and purpose finds fulfilment in the presence of the divine."

Yeshua's gaze turned toward the expansive view before them as he began to unfold the parable of the Bread of Life—a narrative rich with symbolism and spiritual significance.

"In the multitude of people gathered on the hillsides," Yeshua started, "there were those who hungered not just for physical sustenance but for a deeper, more profound nourishment. They sought not ordinary bread but the Bread of Life."

Adeline envisioned the scene—the crowd eager, expectant, and Yeshua standing before them, embodying the essence of the spiritual sustenance they craved.

"I spoke to them," Yeshua continued, "declaring that I am the Bread of Life. Just as physical bread nourishes the body, I am the spiritual sustenance that feeds the hunger of the soul. Whoever comes to me will never hunger, and whoever believes in me will never thirst."

Adeline felt the weight of those words—the promise of spiritual nourishment that transcended the transient needs of the physical body.

"Bread is a universal symbol," Yeshua explained. "It is the staple of life, providing sustenance and energy. In the same way, I offer a sustenance that goes beyond the physical realm—a spiritual nourishment that fills the void within, addressing the deeper longings of the heart."

He gestured towards the nearby mountainside, where the sun cast a warm glow. "Your hunger, Adeline, is not just for ordinary fulfilment. It is a soul-deep longing for meaning, purpose, and connection. I am the Bread of Life that satisfies the spiritual hunger, offering a banquet of grace and love that nourishes the depths of your being."

As Yeshua spoke, Adeline sensed the profound invitation—the call to partake in the Bread of Life, to taste and see that the divine is good.

"The Bread of Life is not bound by the constraints of earthly limitations," Yeshua continued. "It is a feast that transcends time and circumstance, inviting you to partake in the abundance of divine love and wisdom. Your hunger finds fulfilment not in the transient pleasures of the world but in the enduring sustenance of the spiritual journey."

Adeline absorbed the significance of the parable—the assurance that in her seeking, the Bread of Life awaited, offering a feast of spiritual nourishment that would sustain her on the journey of faith.

"May you feast upon me, the Bread of Life," Yeshua concluded, "and find in me, the fulfilment of your deepest longings—a sustenance that not only satisfies the hunger of today but nourishes the eternal journey of your soul."

As they reached a quiet spot within the fortress, Yeshua turned to Adeline, his presence a gentle embrace, and the fortress bore witness to a sacred exchange between the seeker and the divine.

"Adeline," Yeshua spoke, his voice a melodic resonance in the mountain breeze, "this ancient fortress is not just a place of revelation; it is a sanctuary of the soul. Here, in the presence of the sacred, you have glimpsed the profound tapestry of your own journey—a journey intricately connected to our own narrative unfolding through the ages."

Adeline, her heart stirred by the depth of the revelations, met Yeshua's gaze with a mixture of gratitude and wonder.

"In your seeking, you have discovered not just stories but the living, breathing essence of faith—the Lost Sheep, the Prodigal Son, the Mustard Seed, the Samaritan Woman at the Well, and the Bread of Life. Each tale reflects the nuances of your own quest, the yearning of your heart, and the promise of our divine connection that transcends the limitations of human understanding."

Yeshua extended his hand, inviting Adeline to a moment of quiet contemplation. Adeline, feeling the weight of Yeshua's hand, embraced the moment, allowing the echoes of the sacred stories to resonate within her.

"Your faith," Yeshua continued, "is a unique melody, a song that harmonizes with the rhythms of creation. As you descend from this fortress, carry with you the assurance that our presence goes before you, walks beside you, and remains within you—a constant companion on the journey of the soul."

A profound silence enveloped them, broken only by the sands blowing and the distant echoes of the mountain range beside them. Adeline, sensing the completion of this sacred exchange, felt a deep peace settling within.

"May the stories shared on this fortress," Yeshua concluded, "become the chapters of a narrative that unfolds with grace, love, and the timeless presence of the divine. This setting is a beginning, not an end—a sacred marker on the journey that leads you ever closer to our heart."

Adeline and Yeshua stood quietly together, the weight of the stories they had shared hanging in the air like a gentle mist. The fortress, now bathed in the soft glow of the setting sun, felt like a sanctuary, a place where the ancient past and the eternal present met.

"Thank you, Yeshua," Adeline said softly, her voice filled with gratitude. "These stories have always been dear to me, but hearing them from you, here and now, makes them feel more real than ever. I feel like I'm part of them, like they're part of me."

Yeshua smiled, a smile full of love and understanding. "You are part of them, Adeline. These stories are not just about people who lived long ago—they are about you, about every soul that seeks the divine, every heart that yearns for the Father's love. The parables are alive, woven into the very fabric of your life."

Adeline nodded, absorbing his words. She felt a connection to these ancient stories, a sense of belonging to the larger narrative of Papa's love and redemption. The fortress, with its ancient walls and weathered stones, seemed to echo this truth, standing as a silent testament to the enduring power of the stories Yeshua had shared.

After a few moments of silent reflection, Adeline spoke again, her voice filled with a new resolve. "I know I still have much to learn, much to understand. But I feel ready now, ready to embrace my journey, to walk the path that has been laid out for me."

Yeshua's gaze softened, his eyes filled with pride. "You are ready, Adeline. Remember, your journey is unique, but you are never alone. Papa is always with you, guiding your steps, carrying you when you need it. And these stories—let them be your companions, your guideposts along the way."

Adeline took a deep breath, feeling a sense of purpose and clarity that she hadn't felt before. The fortress, once a place of mystery and history, had become a place of revelation, a sacred space where she had encountered the living truth of Papa's love.

As the last rays of the sun dipped below the horizon, Yeshua turned to Adeline, his expression gentle but serious. "It's time to go, Adeline. Your journey is calling you."

Adeline nodded, feeling a mix of emotions—sadness at leaving this holy place, but also excitement and anticipation for what lay ahead. She knew that her journey was far from over, that there were still challenges to face, truths to uncover, and a path to walk that would bring her closer to the Father.

"Where do I go from here?" Adeline asked, her voice steady despite the uncertainty of what lay ahead.

Yeshua smiled, a smile full of love and confidence. "Trust in Us, Adeline. We will show you the way. The road may not always be clear, but know that you are on the right path. Walk in faith, with love in your heart, and you will find your way."

Adeline nodded, feeling the truth of his words resonate deep within her. She knew that the journey ahead would not be easy, but she also knew that she was not alone. The stories Yeshua had shared, the lessons she had learned, and the love of the Father would be her guides, her companions on this sacred journey.

As they began to walk back through the fortress, Adeline took one last look at the ancient walls, the weathered stones that had witnessed so much history, so much of the divine narrative. She felt a deep sense of gratitude for this place, for the revelations it had brought, and for the sacred encounters she had experienced.

When they reached the edge of the fortress, where the ancient stones met the modern world, Yeshua turned to Adeline one last time. "Remember, Adeline, Papa's love is boundless, his grace infinite. No matter where your journey takes you, no matter how far you may wander, you are always welcome in his embrace."

Adeline's eyes filled with tears, not of sadness but of overwhelming love and gratitude. "Thank you, Yeshua," she whispered. "Thank you for everything."

Yeshua smiled, his eyes full of love. "Go in peace, Adeline. Your journey is just beginning."

As Adeline prepared to leave the sacred fortress, a deep sense of gratitude washed over her. She turned to Yeshua, her heart swelling with emotion. "Thank you," she whispered, her voice trembling with awe. "Thank you for this beautiful audience, for allowing me to truly experience you."

Yeshua smiled, his eyes filled with love and understanding. He opened his arms, inviting her into an embrace. As they held each other, Adeline felt the warmth of his presence, and when she looked, she saw the scars in his hands and feet—visible reminders of his sacrifice. Tears welled up in her eyes as she gently touched the marks, her heart overflowing with gratitude and reverence.

"I am with you always, Adeline," Yeshua said softly, his voice comforting. "These scars are a testament to my love for you and all who seek Papa. Carry this moment with you, and know that you are never alone."

Adeline nodded, her heart filled with a deep, abiding peace. She knew that this encounter would remain with her forever, a source of strength and comfort as she continued her journey. As they parted, she felt the imprint of his love, knowing that it would guide her every step.

With those words, Yeshua turned and began to walk away, his figure slowly disappearing into the soft twilight. Adeline watched him go, feeling a profound sense of peace and purpose settle over her.

With one last look at the ancient fortress, Adeline turned and began to walk down the path that led back to the world. The sky above was filled with stars, each one a tiny beacon of light, a reminder of Papa's love that guided her steps.

As she continued on, the journey ahead no longer seemed daunting but was instead filled with hope, purpose, and the promise of divine companionship. Adeline knew that the path she was on would lead her closer to the heart of Papa the Father, and with each step, she embraced the journey with faith and courage, ready to face whatever the future held.

12

The Letting Go

As Adeline descended from the ancient fortress, she felt a profound transformation unfolding within her. The sacred exchange with Yeshua had loosened the grip of past hurts, and the burden she had carried for so long seemed to melt away. The scars of pain and unanswered questions that once weighed her down were being replaced by a liberating sense of peace.

With each step, Adeline felt the presence of Yeshua walking beside her, not as a distant promise but as a living, breathing reality. The journey they shared became a dance—a dance of healing, release, and trust. The wounds of the past were not forgotten but were now being transformed into sources of strength and resilience. She knew that these scars, once symbols of her pain, were now markers of her journey toward healing and wholeness.

Yeshua, sensing the liberation within her spirit, spoke words of encouragement that resonated deep within her soul. "In the letting go, Adeline, you make space for the wondrous unknown. The past, with its pains and disappointments, no longer defines you. Together, we step into the embrace of the divine mystery, where every step is a dance of trust and every breath is a melody of grace."

Adeline relished this newfound freedom. For so long, she had been burdened by the weight of unanswered questions, by the scars of her past. But now, in the company of Yeshua, she found solace, strength, and the courage to explore the depths of love that surrounded her. The freedom she was experiencing was a gift—a precious gift that she cherished deeply. It was a freedom to be herself, to trust in the divine plan, and to step boldly into the future.

"In the wondrous unknown," Yeshua whispered to her soul, "there is a canvas awaiting the brushstrokes of your journey. Papa, like a master artist, is at work in every moment, painting a masterpiece that reflects the beauty of your soul. Trust, dear Adeline, and let each step be a brushstroke, each breath a note in the symphony of your sacred dance."

Adeline knew that there were still many questions left unanswered, mysteries yet to be unravelled, but for now, she embraced the freedom she was experiencing. She relished the joy of simply being in the moment, of walking with Yeshua, and of feeling the burden of her past lift from her shoulders. She was aware that the journey ahead would not be without challenges, but with Yeshua by her side, she felt ready to face whatever lay ahead.

The wondrous unknown, once a source of anxiety and fear, now became a playground of possibilities—a realm where faith, guided by Papa's hand, unfolded in ways beyond her imagination. Adeline, with Yeshua in her heart and by her side, embraced the journey ahead with a heart unburdened and a spirit set free. She was ready to explore the wondrous unknown, to step into the future with courage and hope, and to trust that each moment, each step, was leading her closer to the divine plan that had been crafted for her life.

And so, with a renewed sense of purpose and a deep wellspring of joy, Adeline continued her journey, ready to embrace whatever the future held, confident that she was walking in the light of Papa's love, with Yeshua as her constant companion and guide.

13

The Celts

As the wind carried the scent of the sea, Adeline stood on the rugged cliffs of the Scottish Highlands, feeling the ancient pulse of the land beneath her feet. The mist swirled around her, like a veil between worlds, carrying whispers of her ancestors. She closed her eyes, allowing the elements to speak, each breath reminding her of the rich tapestry of history into which she was woven.

"Te Ata Whetu," Adeline began, her voice steady yet tinged with the weight of her thoughts, "I feel the depth of my Celtic roots, the strength and resilience they represent. But how do I reconcile this with my faith in Yeshua? The Celts were deeply entrenched in pagan practices, in a worldview that feels so far removed from the teachings of scripture."

Te Ata Whetu, standing beside her, turned her gaze to Adeline. Her eyes, filled with timeless understanding, offered gentle reassurance. "Adeline, every culture, every people group, has been touched by Papa's hand. The Celts, like many ancient civilizations, sought to understand the world around them and to connect with the divine in the ways they knew how. Their reverence for nature, respect for the cycles of life, and pursuit of higher knowledge all reflect a yearning for something greater—a yearning that, in its truest form, aligns with the pursuit of truth found in Yeshua."

The angelic guide's voice softened with tenderness. "You see, the Celts lived in a time before the message of Yeshua reached their shores. Their practices, while different from what you now know, were their way of navigating a mysterious world. Papa, in His infinite wisdom, wove a redemptive thread through their culture, just as He has done with all peoples."

Adeline listened intently, her heart beginning to open to the idea that perhaps her Celtic roots were not as opposed to her faith as she had once thought. "But how do I honour this heritage without compromising my beliefs?"

Te Ata Whetu smiled. "It is not about compromise, Adeline, but about integration. The Celts' connection to nature, their sense of community, and their artistry—all these things can be embraced and celebrated as part of your identity. But as you do, let Yeshua be the lens through which you view them. Let His teachings guide you in discerning what to hold onto and what to let go."

The landscape before them began to shift, the mist parting to reveal a lush, green valley dotted with ancient stones. Some stood tall like sentinels, others were half-buried in the earth, remnants of a time long past. The stones, weathered by centuries of wind and rain, bore intricate carvings—spirals, knots, and symbols that pulsed with a life of their own.

"These stones," Te Ata Whetu said, her voice filled with reverence, "are a testament to the Celts' connection to the land and the divine. They believed that sacred sites like these were 'thin spaces' where the physical and spiritual worlds met. Their understanding of the divine may have been incomplete, but their longing for connection with something greater was real and profound."

Adeline walked closer to the stones, tracing the carvings with her fingers. "So, they were searching for Papa, even if they didn't know Him by name?"

"Exactly," Te Ata Whetu affirmed. "When Yeshua's message reached these shores, it resonated with the Celts, fulfilling their deepest yearnings. The transition from pagan practices to the teachings of Yeshua wasn't easy, but many saw the truth in His words—a truth that reflected the same reverence for life and creation that they had always held."

Adeline pondered these words. "Te Ata Whetu, I want to understand more about how Christianity took root in these lands. How did the message of Yeshua reach the Celts? And what role did the saints play in shaping their faith?"

Te Ata Whetu smiled warmly. "Ah, Adeline, that is a story woven with grace and perseverance. The Celts, with their rich spiritual traditions, were not strangers to the divine. It was through the message of Yeshua, however, that they found the light that would guide their faith. The story of how Christianity took root in Wales, Ireland, and Scotland is one of great transformation and dedication. Let us begin with the early Welsh Christians, among the first to hear the Good News."

"In Wales, Christianity likely arrived as early as the second century, though it truly took hold in the fourth and fifth centuries, as Roman influence waned and missionaries spread the gospel across the land. One of the most famous early Welsh saints was Saint David, or Dewi Sant. Born in the late 5th century, Saint David became a central figure in Welsh Christianity. He established a monastery in Glyn Rhosyn, now St. David's in Pembrokeshire, where he taught simplicity, humility, and devotion to Papa."

Te Ata Whetu's voice filled with reverence. "Saint David emphasized prayer, fasting, and preaching the Word of God. He and his monks lived off the land, working manually and praying diligently. David became a unifying figure, helping to spread Christianity while preserving the unique Welsh culture. His famous saying, 'Do the little things,' reminds us of the importance of humility in our walk with Papa. Saint David's legacy continues to inspire believers in Wales to this day."

Adeline nodded, reflecting on the simplicity and dedication of Saint David's life. "It's incredible how one person could have such a lasting impact."

"Indeed," Te Ata Whetu smiled. "But David was not alone. Many others followed his path of devotion, spreading the light of Yeshua in the Celtic world."

"In Ireland, Christianity took root through the work of early saints, the most famous being Saint Patrick. Though born in Roman Britain, Patrick was kidnapped by Irish raiders and brought to Ireland as a slave. After years of captivity, he escaped but later felt a divine calling to return to Ireland as a missionary."

Adeline listened intently. "He used the shamrock to explain the Trinity, didn't he?"

"Yes," Te Ata Whetu confirmed. "Patrick had a deep love for the Irish people, and he used familiar symbols like the shamrock to explain complex Christian teachings. He preached about the Father, Son, and Holy Spirit, and over time, his efforts led to the Christianization of much of Ireland. Patrick's legacy was one of love and persistence, not violence. He built churches, established monasteries, and ordained priests who continued to spread the gospel."

Te Ata Whetu added, "Another significant figure in Irish Christianity was Saint Brigid of Kildare. Known for her deep compassion, Brigid tirelessly worked for the poor. She founded a monastery at Kildare, which became one of the most important centres of learning and faith in Ireland. Brigid's generosity and her commitment to serving others reflected Yeshua's love in action."

Adeline was moved by the depth of compassion in Brigid's life. "It's amazing how these saints not only preached the gospel but lived it out through their actions."

"Exactly," Te Ata Whetu affirmed. "Their lives were living testimonies to the transforming power of the gospel."

Turning northward, Te Ata Whetu spoke of Scotland. "In Scotland, the message of Yeshua was spread by several key figures, most notably Saint Columba. Columba, born in Ireland, left his homeland to bring the gospel to the Picts of Scotland. In

563 AD, he founded the famous monastery on the Isle of Iona, which became a centre for Christian learning and evangelism."

"Iona," Adeline whispered, feeling a connection to the sacred island.

"Yes," Te Ata Whetu said gently. "Iona became a beacon of light in a world darkened by ignorance and violence. From this island, Columba and his monks spread Christianity throughout Scotland. Columba was known for his wisdom, his ability to reconcile warring tribes, and his deep devotion to prayer and study."

"There were others, too," Te Ata Whetu continued. "Saint Ninian, who is often considered the first to bring Christianity to Scotland, and Saint Mungo, who founded the city of Glasgow. Each of these saints planted seeds of faith in the Celtic lands, seeds that grew into a rich and vibrant Christian tradition."

Adeline was quiet for a moment, reflecting on the profound impact these saints had on her ancestors. "It's incredible to think that despite the differences in culture, these saints brought the same message of Yeshua to the people—the same message that has shaped my own faith."

"Yes, Adeline," Te Ata Whetu agreed. "The gospel transcends all cultures and traditions. It has the power to take root in each place and be expressed in a way that speaks to the heart of a people. The Celts, with their connection to nature and their love for storytelling, blended their traditions with the teachings of Yeshua. Celtic Christianity became known for its unique emphasis on creation, seeing God's beauty reflected in nature. The early Celtic Christians often prayed while walking in nature, sensing Papa's presence in the hills, valleys, wind, and sea."

Adeline's heart swelled with appreciation for her heritage. "It's as though the faith of my ancestors wasn't lost but transformed by Yeshua's light."

"Exactly," Te Ata Whetu said. "Yeshua came not to destroy, but to fulfil. The Celtic saints—Saint David, Saint Patrick, Saint Columba—took the beauty of their culture and infused it with the truth of the gospel. Their faith became a living expression of Papa's love."

"You heard me mention the 'thin spaces' in relation to the Celts, but did you know, that there were and are several 'thin spaces' within Celtic Christianity?" Te Ata Whetu gazed at Adeline with a gentle smile, the air around them still as the weight of ancient wisdom settled between them.

"Adeline, the original Christian Celts had a profound understanding of the divine presence woven into the very fabric of the earth. They believed that certain places, often remote and wild, were where the boundary between heaven and earth grew thin—so thin, in fact, that one could almost reach through and touch the eternal. These were the 'thin spaces,' where the veil between the physical and the spiritual world was fragile, and the presence of God was palpable. The Celts sought these places for contemplation, prayer, and pilgrimage, knowing that in these moments, they could feel the sacred closer than ever."

Te Ata Whetu's voice softened as she spoke of these thin spaces, her words drawing Adeline's mind to distant lands. "Islands like Iona, where Saint Columba built his abbey, and Lindisfarne, where Saint Aidan led others in worship, were such places. The Celts believed that these remote places, often surrounded by nature's beauty and solitude, revealed the deep connection between creation and Creator. Even the rocky heights of Skellig Michael, where monks dwelt on a jagged island off the coast of Ireland, were seen as sacred ground—a place where the distractions of the world fell away, and the soul could breathe the air of eternity. They knew that God's presence wasn't confined to stone buildings but spilled over into the hills, rivers, and seas, waiting to be encountered by those with open hearts."

This caused Adeline to stop and pause. As the sun rose higher, casting its light over the land, Adeline felt a deep connection to the saints who had come before her. "Te Ata Whetu, what can I learn from their lives? How can their legacy shape my walk with Yeshua?"

"Their legacy, Adeline, is one of faithfulness," Te Ata Whetu replied, her voice full of warmth. "They walked in the light of Yeshua, despite challenges. They spread the gospel with love, patience, and purpose. Though they weren't perfect, they followed Yeshua with all their hearts."

Te Ata Whetu placed a gentle hand on Adeline's shoulder. "You, too, are called to walk in that same light. Love Papa with all your heart. Serve others with the compassion of Yeshua. And let your life be a testimony to the power of the gospel, just as theirs was."

Adeline nodded, her heart full of gratitude and purpose. She realized that her faith was part of a greater story—one written long before she was born. The saints of Wales, Ireland, and Scotland had laid the foundation, and now it was her turn to carry the torch, walking the path of faith and light in a world still in need of Yeshua's message.

14

The Vikings

As Adeline absorbed the beauty of her Celtic heritage, the scene shifted once again. Now, she stood on the deck of a Viking longship, the open sea a boundless expanse of adventure. The salt in the air invigorated her senses, filling her with a sense of freedom and possibility.

"Feel the salt in the air, Adeline," Te Ata Whetu continued, "for your Viking roots sail with the winds of exploration. The Vikings, fierce warriors and skilled navigators, have passed down to you a spirit of fearlessness and a love for the open sea. Your ancestors, like the Vikings, were adventurers, embracing the unknown with courage."

Adeline stood on the sturdy deck of the Viking longship, her hair whipping in the salty breeze as the vessel cut through the open sea. The horizon stretched endlessly before her, and the rhythmic creaking of the ship seemed to echo the heartbeat of her Viking ancestry.

"Te Ata Whetu, Vikings?" Adeline questioned, her eyes widening with curiosity.

The guide nodded, a glint of excitement in her eyes. "Indeed, my adventurous one. The Vikings were a seafaring people hailing from the Scandinavian regions—Norway, Denmark, and Sweden. They were more than just fierce warriors; they were master navigators, traders, and explorers who left an indelible mark on history."

As Adeline absorbed the vastness of the open sea, Te Ata Whetu began to paint a vivid picture of the Vikings and their way of life.

"The Vikings, much like the Celts, were deeply connected to nature," the guide explained. "But instead of misty hills and serene landscapes, their affinity lay with the boundless expanse of the sea. They were expert shipbuilders, crafting longships that could navigate both open waters and shallow rivers, allowing them to reach far-off lands and explore uncharted territories."

Adeline felt a surge of pride as she imagined her Viking ancestors, fearless and skilled, setting sail on daring voyages. The angelic guide continued, "The Vikings were not only warriors; they were traders who established trade routes extending from the British Isles to the Mediterranean. They bartered goods, exchanged cultures, and left their mark on distant lands, contributing to the rich tapestry of world history."

"Their sense of adventure was unparalleled," Te Ata Whetu emphasized. "Driven by a desire to discover new lands and seek out opportunities, they ventured as far as North America, long before Columbus set foot on the continent. The open sea was both their playground and their livelihood, a testament to their courage and resilience."

Adeline felt the salt in the air, the same salt that clung to the skin of her Viking ancestors as they faced the challenges of the open sea. "Fearlessness," Te Ata Whetu continued, "was a trait they passed down through generations—a spirit that embraced the unknown with courage and determination."

The angelic guide's gaze fixed on the distant horizon. "So, my dear Adeline, just as your Celtic roots connect you to the misty hills and ancient traditions, your Viking roots bind you to the thrill of exploration and the boundless sea. Embrace the adventurous spirit of your ancestors, for it is a legacy of fearlessness that can guide you through the uncharted waters of life."

As Adeline stood on the Viking longship, she felt a profound connection to the seafaring heritage that unfolded before her. The spirit of the Vikings, with their sails billowing in the wind, beckoned her to embrace the vastness of adventure that lay on the horizon.

But a shadow of doubt crossed her mind, and Adeline turned to Te Ata Whetu with a furrowed brow. "Te Ata Whetu, that all sounds amazing, but I have one question for you. How can I embrace this part of my heritage knowing how brutal and vengeful the Vikings were? Weren't they notorious for raping and pillaging villages that they wanted to conquer, as well as being brutes of maleficent violence too?"

Te Ata Whetu sighed, acknowledging the complexity of the question. "Adeline, it's true that the Vikings had a reputation for raids and conquests, and the historical accounts often highlight the violent aspects of their activities. However, it's crucial to approach our understanding of history with a nuanced perspective."

She took a moment before continuing, "While it's undeniable that some Viking expeditions involved raiding, raping, and pillaging, it's essential to recognise that this wasn't the entirety of their culture. Vikings were also skilled traders, explorers, and settlers. Their motivations were diverse, driven by a quest for resources, trade opportunities, and even the pursuit of new lands for settlement."

Te Ata Whetu walked to the ship's edge, gazing out at the vast sea. "In history, narratives often focus on the sensational, on the conflicts and the extraordinary. However, the everyday lives of the Vikings were multifaceted. They had communities, families, and societal structures that encompassed more than just warfare."

Adeline, accepting the guide's willingness to convey a balanced perspective, asked, "So, how do I reconcile this duality? The adventurous, exploratory side with the more brutal aspects of Viking history?"

Te Ata Whetu turned back to Adeline, her expression thoughtful. "Embracing your Viking heritage doesn't mean endorsing or glorifying violence. Instead, it involves acknowledging the entirety of their legacy—the good and the challenging. Learn from their mistakes and misdeeds, understanding the historical context that shaped their actions."

Te Ata Whetu continued, "Seek to embody the positive aspects of their spirit—the courage, resilience, and curiosity—while actively rejecting the darker elements. Remember that heritage is not a static concept; it evolves as we reinterpret and understand it in the context of our own values and beliefs."

Adeline nodded, absorbing her guide's words. "In doing so," Te Ata Whetu added, "you contribute to reshaping the narrative, emphasizing the richness of your heritage beyond the stereotypes. Use the knowledge of both the triumphs and shortcomings of your ancestors to cultivate a sense of responsibility and a commitment to a more enlightened path."

Te Ata Whetu stepped closer, her voice soft yet firm. "Adeline, you can look to scripture as your guiding light, your plumb line, as you navigate the complexities of your heritage. The teachings of Yeshua emphasize love, mercy, and compassion—qualities that stand in stark contrast to the violence that marked parts of Viking history. By filtering your understanding of your ancestors through the lens of scripture, you can honour what is good and true while rejecting what goes against the teachings of Yeshua."

She continued, "Consider how Yeshua transformed those who followed Him. Just as He called fishermen, tax collectors, and zealots to become His disciples and taught them a new way of living, so too can you take the positive attributes of your Viking ancestors—like their bravery, their adventurous spirit, and their resilience—and let those be transformed by the light of Yeshua's teachings. This transformation doesn't erase their history but redeems it, allowing you to carry forward a heritage that is aligned with your faith."

As the ship sailed on, Adeline contemplated the complexity of her Viking heritage. It was a legacy that demanded introspection, understanding, and a conscious effort to build upon the positive aspects while learning from the mistakes of the past.

The sea carried the scent of adventure, and Adeline's excitement grew as she embraced the heritage of her Viking lineage. Yet, the journey was not complete. She realized that, just as her Viking ancestors braved the unknown, she too must navigate the uncharted waters of her own identity, guided by the light of Yeshua and the wisdom of her ancestors.

Together, Adeline and Te Ata Whetu stood at the bow of the ship, the horizon stretching before them. The past, with all its complexities, had shaped her, but the future was hers to navigate. And as she sailed forward, Adeline knew that she could honour her heritage while walking in the path of righteousness, a path illuminated by the love and teachings of Yeshua.

15

Islands of the Sea

"Now," Te Ata Whetu declared, "let us voyage to the Polynesian islands, where the sea is not just a barrier but a highway. Your Polynesian voyager side, with its navigational prowess and connection to the vast Pacific, is another chapter of your heritage. The ocean, in its rhythmic dance, has been a guide for your ancestors, leading them to new lands and new beginnings."

Adeline stood on the shores of a Polynesian island, the warmth of the sun and the rhythmic beat of drums echoing in the air. The sea, crystal clear, whispered stories of migration and discovery.

She felt the soft warmth of the sand beneath her feet as she stood on the shores of the Polynesian island, captivated by the beauty of the turquoise waters stretching out before her. Te Ata Whetu's words resonated with the rhythmic beat of drums in the air, and she could almost feel the pulse of her Polynesian heritage vibrating through the land.

"Te Ata Whetu," Adeline asked, "tell me more about my Polynesian voyager side. What stories do the sea and the islands hold for our family?"

The guide smiled, her eyes reflecting the pride of shared tales. "The Polynesians, my dear, were master navigators and seafarers. Across the vastness of the Pacific, they embarked on daring voyages using celestial navigation, the stars, and the patterns of ocean currents as their guides. The sea wasn't just a barrier—it was a highway connecting distant islands."

She gestured toward the horizon, where a traditional Polynesian outrigger canoe gracefully cut through the water. "Your ancestors, with unmatched navigational prowess, explored the Pacific long before the arrival of European explorers. They traversed thousands of miles, discovering and settling on islands across the vast expanse of the ocean."

Adeline's eyes followed the canoe, imagining the courageous voyages of her Polynesian forebears. "Their connection to the sea wasn't merely practical; it was deeply spiritual. The ocean was a living entity, a force that linked them to their ancestors and provided sustenance for their communities. The art of wayfinding was a sacred tradition, passed down through generations."

"The rhythm of drums you hear," Te Ata Whetu continued, "is not just a musical expression but a cultural heartbeat. Polynesians used drumming not only for communication but also to celebrate milestones, tell stories, and honour their gods. The beats echoed across the islands, a unifying language that bound the Polynesian people together."

As Adeline absorbed the richness of her Polynesian heritage, she noticed the vibrant colours of traditional clothing, the intricate tattoos on the skin of the islanders, and the lush greenery that surrounded her. "Polynesian societies," Te Ata Whetu explained, "were structured around communal living, with a strong emphasis on respect for nature and the interconnectedness of all living things."

She walked with Adeline along the shore, sharing stories of the hula dances that celebrated both the beauty of the islands and the struggles of life. "The hula," Te Ata Whetu said, "is not just a dance; it's a form of storytelling, a way to pass down history and cultural knowledge from one generation to the next."

Adeline closed her eyes, feeling the warmth of the sun on her face and the gentle breeze carrying the essence of the Pacific. "Your Polynesian roots," her guide concluded, "are a celebration of navigation, community, and a profound connection to the sea. As you stand here, let the stories of your Polynesian ancestors guide you on a journey of discovery and appreciation for the diverse chapters of your heritage."

Adeline, reflecting on the beauty and depth of her Polynesian roots, found herself once again grappling with the tension between her faith and the cultural practices of her ancestors. "Again, Te Ata Whetu, how do I reconcile a culture that worships all these different gods, instead of Papa, the One True God? I'm not trying to be difficult, just trying to understand all the different aspects that make up me!" Adeline chuckled to herself. "How is Papa okay with them worshipping other gods when the Ten Commandments explicitly say not to?"

Te Ata Whetu's eyes reflected a deep understanding of Adeline's inner struggle. She paused, choosing her words with care. "Adeline, your question touches upon a profound aspect of faith and cultural diversity. It's important to recognise that as believers in Yeshua, we believe in the One True God, and that is the foundation of our faith."

Continuing on, "The commandments, including the prohibition against worshipping other gods, are central to our beliefs. They provide a moral and spiritual framework for our relationship with Papa and with one another. However, the coexistence of different beliefs in the world challenges us to approach this complexity with empathy and respect."

Te Ata Whetu walked beside Adeline, the sound of the waves providing a backdrop to their conversation. "In understanding other cultures and their diverse beliefs, it's crucial to approach the question with humility. The cultural and historical contexts in which these beliefs emerged are intricate, and they often offer unique perspectives on the human experience."

Further explaining, "While we, as believers in Yeshua, may firmly hold our faith in the One True God, we can approach the beliefs of others with a spirit of tolerance and a willingness to engage in dialogue. This doesn't mean compromising our own beliefs but rather embracing the diversity of the human journey and acknowledging that people interpret the divine in various ways."

Adeline pondered Te Ata Whetu's words, realizing the delicate balance between upholding one's own faith and respecting the beliefs of others. "Remember," her guide continued, "our faith encourages us to love our neighbours, to seek understanding, and to promote peace. This doesn't mean endorsing other belief systems, but rather engaging with them in a way that fosters mutual respect and acceptance."

Te Ata Whetu smiled gently at Adeline. "Your journey of self-discovery involves navigating these complex waters. Embrace the values that guide your faith, and, in doing so, be a beacon of love and understanding in a world marked by diversity. It's a delicate dance, my dear, but one that allows you to appreciate the unique aspects of your heritage while upholding the principles that anchor your true identity."

Adeline nodded, appreciating the wisdom in her guide's words. As they continued their walk along the shore, she felt a sense of peace, knowing that her journey of understanding would be a continuous exploration of faith, identity, and the interconnectedness of the diverse aspects that made up her heritage.

"Te Ata Whetu," Adeline marvelled, "it's like the sea is in my DNA, connecting all these pieces of my heritage. What a beautiful, intricate tapestry!"

"Precisely, Adeline," her guide affirmed. "The sea, with its ebb and flow, mirrors the journey of your ancestors. Embrace the fluidity of your heritage, for within it, you carry the strength of the Celtic cliffs, the adventurous spirit of the Viking longships, and the navigational wisdom of Polynesian canoes. The sea unites these stories, and you, my dear, are the culmination of their journeys."

As Adeline stood at the crossroads of her heritage, she felt a profound sense of gratitude and belonging. The sea, in all its forms, was a living testament to the resilience and courage imprinted in her DNA—a heritage that spanned continents and ages.

With Te Ata Whetu as her angelic guide, Adeline eagerly continued the exploration of her ancestral roots, ready to uncover more layers of the tapestry that defined her identity.

16

The Stone

Adeline stood on the shore, her breaths still heavy from the underwater journey that had brought her to this moment. The early morning sun began to rise, casting its golden light over the horizon and turning the ocean into a shimmering expanse. She could still feel the coolness of the water on her skin, but in her hand, something warm pulsed with life. The stone she had found on the ocean floor, small and smooth, carried a warmth that grew with each passing second. Its intricate spiral carvings seemed to shift and glow as the sunlight hit them, as though they were alive with a purpose she had yet to fully understand.

Te Ata Whetu, her angelic guide, stood beside her, silent for a moment, before her voice, resonating with the authority of heaven, broke the stillness. "You've done well, Adeline," she said, her eyes filled with pride. "The stone you hold is a key—a connection to your spiritual heritage and a guide on the path Papa has set before you. In time, you'll understand more."

Adeline, now fully present, looked down at the stone once more, feeling the weight of its significance. The spiral etched into its surface wasn't just an ancient symbol; it was a connection to her ancestors—the Celts, the Vikings, and the Maori. These were three distinct cultures, separated by vast oceans and centuries, yet all were united by the spiral, a powerful symbol with deep spiritual meaning.

Te Ata Whetu gestured toward the stone, her voice taking on a reflective tone. "The spiral is a symbol that has echoed across time, Adeline. To the Celts, it was the journey of life itself —the never-ending cycles of birth, death, and rebirth. They saw life as a continuous loop, each stage of existence feeding into the next, a path of spiritual growth that led ever closer to the divine. The spiral symbolized their understanding of the eternal nature of the soul, always moving forward, always returning to the Source."

Adeline could almost see her Celtic ancestors, with their deep reverence for nature and the divine, carving spirals into their stones and weaving them into their art, all as a way to honor the journey of life. Their belief in a world where the spiritual and the physical intertwined felt so similar to her own experiences— the 'thin spaces' where she felt closest to Papa.

Te Ata Whetu's gaze shifted slightly, and she continued. "And then, your Viking ancestors—the spiral held power for them too. For the Vikings, it represented the movement of the soul between the worlds of the living and the dead. They saw existence as a series of interconnected realms, and the spiral was a map of those realms, with each turn marking a passage through life, death, and beyond."

Adeline imagined her Viking forebears, fierce and unyielding, sailing across rough seas with that same spiral etched into the prow of their ships. It was a symbol not only of life's journey but of resilience, of pushing forward through every storm and trial. The trials she had faced in her own life felt connected to this—the battles she had fought, both internal and external, had shaped her path, and like the Vikings, she had emerged stronger each time.

"The spiral, for them, was a symbol of strength," Te Ata Whetu said softly. "To endure life's hardships, to battle against the odds, and to rise again with new wisdom—that is what the Vikings understood so well."

Adeline nodded, feeling the weight of the stone in her hand shift slightly. She knew that the spiral was more than a symbol of her heritage. It represented the trials she had faced and the way her faith had carried her through each one. Every difficulty had been another turn in the spiral, drawing her ever closer to the light of Heaven.

Finally, Te Ata Whetu turned her gaze toward the horizon, as if summoning the ancient wisdom of the Maori people. "The spiral—or the koru, as it is called in Maori culture—is a sacred symbol, one that speaks of life, growth, and renewal. Just as the fern uncurls as it grows, so too does the koru represent the unfolding of new life, the constant evolution of the soul as it returns to its roots."

Adeline smiled, memories of her upbringing among the Maori flashing through her mind. She had always been surrounded by the koru—in art, in the carvings of the meeting houses, and even in the tattoos of her people. The koru was a symbol of peace, of strength, of balance. It was a reminder that life was always moving forward, but that it also returned, again and again, to its beginnings. It was about finding harmony in the cycles of existence.

Te Ata Whetu nodded at the thoughts forming in Adeline's mind. "Your Maori ancestors believed that balance was key—living in harmony with the land, the sea, and the divine. The koru was a reminder that while life constantly evolves, it also remains grounded in the past, in tradition, in faith. It teaches that growth comes from staying connected to your roots, to the source of strength that is found in faith and in Papa."

Adeline looked down at the stone once more, feeling its warmth spread through her fingertips. The koru, like the spiral of the Celts and the Vikings, was a symbol of the path she was on, a path that wasn't always easy but one that was filled with purpose. The stone wasn't just a connection to her ancestors; it was a tangible reminder of her faith, her journey, and the divine hand that guided her along the way.

Te Ata Whetu stepped closer, her voice taking on a deeper, more reflective tone. "The spiral isn't just a symbol of your past, Adeline. It's a guide for your future. Scripture speaks of life as a journey—Psalm 119:105 reminds us that His word is a lamp to our feet and a light to our path. This spiral represents that path, winding its way forward, always drawing you closer to the light, to Yeshua."

Adeline closed her eyes for a moment, reciting the words in her heart, feeling the truth of them settle deep within her. She had walked this path of faith for so long, through trials and joy, and now, with the stone in her hand, she felt a renewed sense of purpose. The spiral was a symbol of that journey, and she knew she would continue to walk it, always moving forward, always guided by Yeshua's light.

"The stone you hold is a key," Te Ata Whetu repeated, her voice filled with authority. "A reminder that you are part of something much greater than yourself. The spiral is a symbol of your journey, of the cycles of life, of faith, of the unfolding plan that Papa has for you. Hold onto it, Adeline, for it will guide you as you walk the path ahead."

Adeline felt the weight of the stone, not just in her hand but in her soul. It was more than just a symbol—it was a promise, a reminder that her journey with Yeshua would continue to unfold, guided by His love and grace.

She looked up at Te Ata Whetu, her heart full of gratitude. "Thank you," she whispered, her voice filled with emotion. "I feel like I'm finally beginning to understand."

Te Ata Whetu smiled, her eyes glowing with a gentle light. "This is just the beginning, Adeline. Papa has so much more to show you. Each turn in the spiral brings you closer to Him. You are not alone—He is with you, guiding you through every step."

Adeline stood still for a moment, letting the words wash over her. The sun had now fully risen, casting its light over the ocean, and in that light, she felt a deep sense of peace. She knew that the journey ahead would not always be easy, but with Yeshua as her anchor, she would walk it with confidence, knowing that every step was part of a greater plan.

The stone in her hand pulsed with warmth once more, as if it, too, held the promise of what was to come.

17

Island Dream

As the sun dipped below the horizon, casting hues of orange and pink across the sky, Adeline found herself standing with Te Ata Whetu at the edge of the lush garden, where Nani often spent her evenings. The air was filled with the fragrance of tropical blooms, and the sound of the ocean waves provided a gentle backdrop to the moment.

Te Ata Whetu, with a twinkle in her eyes, took Adeline's hand and led her toward a weathered stone bench nestled under the swaying palm trees. A beautiful older lady, with her silver hair glowing in the twilight, looked up from a book of ancient Polynesian tales she was reading.

"Nani," Te Ata Whetu said with a warmth that echoed through the garden, "I want you to meet someone very special. This is Adeline, your granddaughter."

Nani's eyes sparkled with recognition and curiosity as she closed the book and stood up. Adeline felt a mix of excitement and reverence, standing before this woman who held a connection to a shared ancestry.

"Adeline," Te Ata Whetu continued, "Nani is not just a storyteller; she's a keeper of our history, a bridge between the past and the present."

Adeline nodded, feeling a sense of responsibility and privilege in meeting Nani. She had heard tales of her ancient foremother from Te Ata Whetu but seeing her in person, with the wisdom etched into the lines on her face, was a different experience altogether.

Nani approached Adeline and, with a traditional Polynesian greeting, gently pressed her forehead against Adeline's. "Haere mai, my dear. You carry the spirit of our people within you."

Adeline, moved by the gesture, reciprocated the greeting, feeling an immediate connection that transcended time. Nani's eyes held a depth of knowledge, and Adeline sensed that beneath the surface of this meeting lay a tapestry of stories waiting to be unravelled.

Te Ata Whetu stepped back, allowing the two women to have their moment. Nani, with a warm smile, gestured for Adeline to join her on the stone bench. As they sat together under the tropical night sky, Nani began to share stories of their ancestors, weaving a narrative that connected Adeline to the roots of her identity.

In that enchanting garden, surrounded by the whispers of the past and the rustling leaves, Adeline embarked on a journey of discovery guided by the ancient wisdom of her foremother, Nani.

As Adeline and Nani sat on the stone bench beneath the tropical night sky, the air was filled with the soothing sounds of nature. Nani, with her silver hair shimmering in the moonlight, couldn't help but notice the inquisitive sparkle in Adeline's eyes.

"Well, well, Adeline," Nani chuckled, "Te Ata Whetu told me you've been digging into our family history. Ready for a few surprises?"

Adeline grinned, appreciating Nani's cheeky demeanour. "I'm all ears, Nani. Lay it on me."

With a mischievous glint in her eyes, Nani leaned in and whispered, "You know, our ancestors were not just skilled navigators. Some of them had a knack for storytelling that could rival even the best stand-up comedians."

Adeline laughed, intrigued by the prospect of a comedic twist to her family's history. Nani continued, "Legend has it that one of our great-great-grandmothers was known for her wit. She could have the entire village in stitches with her tales."

Te Ata Whetu, standing nearby, couldn't help but join the conversation. "Ah yes, your foremother, Te Ruru. She had a way with words that could turn the most serious moments into laughter."

Adeline, now eager to hear more, asked, "Tell me a story about Te Ruru, Nani."

Nani leaned back on the stone bench, a twinkle in her eye. "Well, there's a tale about the time she convinced the entire village that the coconut trees were holding secret meetings after dark. She claimed to have overheard them whispering about the gossip from neighbouring islands!"

Adeline burst into laughter, envisioning coconut trees as clandestine conspirators. "Te Ruru sounds like my kind of ancestor!"

Nani grinned, "Oh, she was a character, alright. Our history is filled with heroes, adventurers, and a fair share of pranksters. It's what makes us who we are."

As the night unfolded, Nani seamlessly blended storytelling and humour, painting a vivid picture of their ancestors who not only navigated the vast Pacific but also embraced the joy and laughter that come with shared moments. Adeline, feeling a deep connection to her roots, realized that the spirit of cheekiness and humour had been passed down through generations.

Underneath the starlit sky, Adeline, Nani, and Te Ata Whetu continued to share stories, weaving together laughter and history, creating a tapestry that celebrated not only the resilience of their people but also the lighthearted moments that added colour to their heritage.

Nani looked at her distant granddaughter and smiled. She had such a cheeky yet wise-looking face and was very excited to be with Adeline. Walking to the garden with the seven stones, she pointed out the plaque to Adeline, who stood there gobsmacked.

"Are you telling me that Tainui stopped here on their way to Aotearoa, New Zealand, Nani?"

"No child, I'm telling you, you have your history all back to front! You are from here. Not some mystical land called Hawaiiki, which coincidentally, is not Hawaii."

Adeline couldn't speak for a few moments. Taking a moment to process this information, she suddenly remembered her

Eema's conversation with her after returning from her honeymoon with her Abba. Her mother had mentioned they had gone on a guided tour. After many times on the island, she had only discovered this garden and its precious stones, commemorating the significant voyage that left Rarotonga centuries ago. Her Eema had known there would come a day when this would be important information for Adeline and Claudine, and now Addie was at the beginning of it.

"So, as a member of the Tainui tribe, I'm actually from The Cook Islands, ancestrally?"

"That is correct, granddaughter. Bit of a trip, eh?" Nani giggled, which made Adeline relax and laugh as well.

"We here, in all these Polynesian Islands, are all interconnected. Sure, our language has changed over the centuries, and some of our customs differ, but we are all related to the core of who we are as people. This means something, Addie, and you must understand this."

Adeline took time to digest this information before asking any more questions and then turned to hug Nani. She had a fondness for this woman and was thankful Te Ata Whetu had allowed them time together.

After some time, the women walked over near the shoreline and looked past the lagoon. This area was one of the few places that sea vessels could leave, with a gap in the lagoon. Most of the island had a ring of coral rock that protected the waters and the island itself.

Having never been here and yet heard all about it from her mother, Adeline was entranced by the lagoon. It seemed to beckon to her and call out in a way she hadn't experienced back home in Aotearoa.

Taking off her jandals and not minding that she was in a t-shirt and shorts, Addie waded into the shallows and was met with beautiful tepid water. She looked down and saw the pristine white sand, along with the rocks and coral, dotted the lagoon's bottom. Looking closer, she saw a beautiful deep velvet blue starfish slowly swim around and was mesmerised. The colours of the sea life seemed to be much brighter and richer in hue than back in her homeland. But to be fair, she hadn't spent time in the water for years, so maybe she had forgotten. But certainly, growing up in the Bay, there wasn't fish around like this! Addie felt extra special and thanked Papa, under her breath.

As she walked deeper into the lagoon, Addie was shocked the water only remained just over her chest. Realising she could walk over to the small islands that inhabited the lagoon, she dove under the water and swam to the island. As she reached the shoreline, she was met by her guide, Te Ata Whetu.

After a moment or two, Nani appeared before her again.

"Oh, that's right. You can morph and move like Papa! I forgot that. How nice to not be constrained by time, space and this earth, Nani!" They giggled again, with Nani giving Addie a towel to dry herself.

Walking around the small island, Adeline was struck by the view and the rugged coastal shoreline at the far side of this atol. She surmised that this and the other two small islands took a lot of the weather and, indeed, a tremendous beating when the weather turned nasty, and cyclones happened upon this place. She then remembered her mother speaking of her first night on this island all those decades again, with her own parents, and how Alexandria had slept through a cyclone the first night. Indeed, when she woke, she was shocked to see all the trees down and the debris everywhere until the staff at the motel shared what had happened. This island, indeed, was stunning but unpredictable. Addie knew she had better not forget this fact.

Adeline continued to explore the small island, taking in the unique flora and fauna that adorned its shores. The air was filled with the sweet scent of tropical flowers, and the sound of waves crashing against the coral reef provided a soothing background melody. Nani followed closely behind, sharing anecdotes about the island's history and its resilience in the face of unpredictable weather.

As they walked, Nani pointed out the remnants of an ancient marae, a sacred Polynesian meeting place, nestled among the coconut palms. Adeline marvelled at the carved stones and the sense of history they exuded. It was a tangible connection to her roots, and she couldn't help but feel a profound respect for the ancestors who had once gathered in this sacred space.

The sun began its descent, casting a warm golden glow over the lagoon. Adeline and Nani found a comfortable spot on the beach to sit and absorb the beauty around them. The sky transformed into a canvas of oranges, pinks, and purples as the day made way for the night. Nani shared stories of the traditional voyages, the navigational skills of the ancestors, and the deep connection Polynesians had with the sea.

As the stars emerged overhead, Nani spoke of the celestial navigation techniques that guided the ancient voyagers across the vast Pacific. Adeline listened intently, feeling a sense of pride in her newfound understanding of her heritage. The night unfolded with tales of bravery, cultural practices, and the importance of preserving the wisdom passed down through generations.

Nani continued to share the stories of their ancestors, she delved into the remarkable navigational skills that set them apart in the vastness of the Pacific. Leaning forward, she spoke with a reverence that reflected the awe-inspiring nature of their forebears.

"Our ancestors, Adeline, were masterful navigators," Nani began, her eyes reflecting the flickering light of a nearby torch. "Long before the days of compasses and GPS, they relied on the stars, the currents, and the flight patterns of migratory birds to traverse the open ocean."

Adeline listened intently, captivated by the idea of ancient voyages guided by the celestial bodies above. Nani continued, "Our people were wayfinders, skilled in the art of celestial navigation. They could read the stars like a map, using constellations as guideposts to navigate the vast expanse of the Pacific."

She gestured towards the night sky, pointing out familiar constellations. "The Southern Cross, for instance, was a crucial marker. It helped them determine their latitude, ensuring they stayed on course. And then there's the rising and setting of certain stars, like Hōkūle'a, which guided them on their journeys."

Nani, her eyes reflecting the wisdom of ages, added, "And it wasn't just the stars. They observed the behaviour of ocean currents, the flight patterns of migratory birds, and the colour and temperature of the water. It was a holistic understanding of the environment that allowed them to navigate with precision."

Adeline marvelled at the depth of knowledge required for such navigation. "It's incredible to think about how they could navigate thousands of miles across the open sea with such accuracy."

Nani nodded, a sense of pride evident in her expression. "Indeed, it was a sacred knowledge passed down from generation to generation. They were not just sailors; they were guardians of the sea, reading its secrets to ensure safe passage."

She continued, "And the wayfinding wasn't just a practical skill; it was deeply intertwined with spirituality. The navigator, or 'pwo,' as they were called, was not only responsible for the crew's safety but also for maintaining a spiritual connection with the ocean and the celestial realm."

Adeline, now fully immersed in the tales of ancient navigation, felt a profound respect for the legacy of her ancestors. "It's not just a skill; it's a sacred art."

Nani nodded in agreement. "Exactly, Adeline. Our ancestors understood that the ocean wasn't just a physical barrier; it was a pathway connecting our islands, our people, and our stories. The navigational skills were a manifestation of that profound connection."

Under the star-studded sky, Adeline couldn't help but feel a deep sense of gratitude for the wisdom of her forebears. The navigational legacy they left behind was not just a testament to their practical prowess but also a spiritual bond that transcended time and space, connecting the past to the present and the present to the future.

Adeline gazed out at the lagoon, now illuminated by the moonlight. The water sparkled like a sea of diamonds, and she felt a profound connection to the land and its people. Nani, sensing Adeline's contemplation, spoke softly, "Our stories are etched into the land and the sea. They are the threads that bind us across time and space. Cherish them, for they are the legacy you carry."

18

Nani's Storytelling

As the night embraced them under the tropical sky, Nani shifted the conversation toward tales of bravery—stories that illuminated the courage and resilience of their ancestors. Adeline, still enthralled by the rich tapestry of her heritage, leaned in eagerly to hear these accounts of valour.

"Adeline, let me tell you about Te Awhiorangi," Nani began, her voice carrying the weight of centuries. "She was a warrior chiefess, a beacon of strength among our people. Legend has it that during a time of tribal conflict when tensions were high and uncertainty loomed, Te Awhiorangi stepped forward with unwavering determination."

Te Ata Whetu, her eyes reflecting the firelight, nodded in agreement. "Te Awhiorangi was not only a skilled warrior but also a charismatic leader. She rallied our people, uniting them against common adversaries. Her fearlessness on the battlefield and her ability to inspire others made her a legendary figure."

Adeline, imagining the scenes of battle and the powerful presence of Te Awhiorangi, asked, "What made her so remarkable?"

Nani smiled, "It wasn't just her prowess with a weapon, although she was a formidable warrior. It was her sense of justice and her commitment to protecting the vulnerable. She fought not just for victory in battle but for the well-being of our people."

Te Ata Whetu added, "Te Awhiorangi believed in the strength of unity. She forged alliances with neighbouring tribes, recognizing that solidarity was key to facing external threats. Her diplomacy was as sharp as her blade."

As the tales unfolded, Nani spoke of another figure, Kahuwai, who faced the perils of the sea in a different kind of battle. "Kahuwai was an expert seafarer, a navigator of great skill. During a treacherous storm that battered our islands, Kahuwai took it upon himself to ensure the safety of his people."

Adeline, with a keen interest in maritime stories, asked, "What did he do?"

Whetu continued, "Kahuwai, without hesitation, set sail into the heart of the storm. He navigated the turbulent waters with a courage that bordered on the divine. Guided by the stars and his deep connection with the sea, he led his people through the tempest to safety."

Te Ata Whetu nodded, "Kahuwai's bravery extended beyond the physical. It was a testament to the trust our people placed in their leaders, and the unwavering belief that, even in the face of the fiercest storms, they would find a way forward."

As the night wore on, Adeline found herself immersed in these tales of bravery—stories that resonated with the spirit of her ancestors. Through Te Awhiorangi's leadership and Kahuwai's seafaring courage, Adeline felt a profound connection to the legacy of resilience that defined their people.

Underneath the starlit canopy, surrounded by the echoes of these ancestral stories, Adeline realized that bravery, in the context of her heritage, wasn't just about facing physical adversaries but also about standing firm in the face of adversity, leading with compassion, and navigating the unpredictable seas of life with unwavering determination.

Nani, noticing Adeline's fascination with the tales of bravery, decided to sprinkle in a few stories of Te Ruru, the mischievous figure who added a touch of humour and lightness to the often intense narratives of their ancestors.

"Ah, Te Ruru!" Nani exclaimed with a twinkle in her eye. "She kept our ancestors on their toes. Te Ruru was a trickster, a jester with a heart full of laughter. Legend has it that during times of solemn ceremonies, Te Ruru couldn't resist injecting a bit of mirth into the proceedings."

Te Ata Whetu chuckled, remembering the antics of Te Ruru. "Te Ruru had a knack for disguises. Once, during a sacred ritual, she managed to sneak into the ceremony disguised as an elder. The elders, not suspecting a thing, were treated to a lively dance that left everyone in stitches."

Adeline grinned, delighted by the thought of a mischievous elder disrupting a solemn ceremony. "What happened when she was found out?"

Nani laughed, "Oh, Te Ruru was quick on her feet. As soon as her true identity was revealed, she vanished into the shadows, leaving behind laughter and a sense of joy. Te Ruru believed that even in the most serious moments, a good laugh could be the balm that heals the soul."

Te Ata Whetu added, "Te Ruru's pranks weren't just for entertainment; they were a reminder not to take life too seriously. During challenges, Te Ruru would appear with a clever joke or a playful trick, lifting the spirits of the people."

As the night continued, Adeline found herself enchanted not only by the tales of bravery and resilience but also by the mischievous antics of Te Ruru. In the grand tapestry of her heritage, Te Ruru added a thread of lightheartedness, reminding Adeline that even in the most challenging moments, a good laugh could be a powerful ally.

19

Over the Centuries

As Adeline stood on the shores of the Cook Islands, the turquoise waters lapping at her feet, Te Ata Whetu, her angelic guide, appeared beside her, radiating a serene yet solemn presence. "Are you ready, Adeline?" she asked, her voice gentle yet imbued with a deep, ancient wisdom.

Adeline nodded, bracing herself as Nani extended her hand. With a flash of light, they were transported back in time to the 19th century. Adeline found herself in a vibrant village on the island of Aitutaki, where the islanders went about their daily lives with joy and reverence for their traditions. The scent of frangipani flowers filled the air, and the rhythmic beat of drums resonated through the trees.

Then, the scene shifted. Adeline watched as the first missionaries from the London Missionary Society arrived, their ships casting long shadows over the island's shore. At first, the missionaries seemed friendly, offering gifts and learning the local customs. They spoke of a new God and a new way of life, promising hope and salvation. The islanders, curious and open-hearted, welcomed these strangers, eager to understand their message.

Adeline observed the missionaries slowly gaining the trust of the islanders. They learned the language, participated in the local ceremonies, and even adopted some of the islanders' customs. The villagers, intrigued by the missionaries' tales of a loving God and eternal life, began to attend their meetings. There was an initial harmony, a blending of cultures that gave Adeline a fleeting sense of hope.

But soon, the atmosphere changed. The missionaries, emboldened by their initial success, began to impose their beliefs more aggressively. They dismantled the sacred meeting houses, the marae, and destroyed the idols and symbols that the islanders held dear. Adeline watched in horror as the missionaries smashed the intricately carved wooden idols, the sacred symbols of the islanders' gods, and set fire to the beautifully adorned marae. The islanders were devastated, their cultural heritage and spiritual symbols trampled underfoot.

Adeline's heart ached as she saw the devastation in the eyes of the islanders. They had opened their homes and hearts to the missionaries, only to have their deepest beliefs shattered. The destruction of their sacred spaces led to an uproar among the islanders. Newly converted islanders, caught in the turmoil of their old beliefs and the new teachings, found themselves in a painful conflict. Families were divided, friends turned against each other, and the peaceful village was thrown into chaos.

The tension escalated into a bloodbath. Adeline witnessed the heartbreaking scenes of violence: the clashes between the islanders and the missionaries, the cries of pain, and the rivers of blood staining the once serene landscape. The village was torn apart, its harmony shattered by the force of cultural collision. Mothers wept over the bodies of their children, warriors defended their heritage with the last of their strength, and elders mourned the desecration of their sacred sites.

The violence left deep scars that echoed through generations. All these years later, the pain and dissension sown by these events still echoed through the generations, creating a rift between the early settlers and the indigenous people. Adeline felt a deep sorrow and anger welling up inside her. This was never meant to be.

Nani's voice broke through her thoughts. "The Bible spoke of making disciples and sharing the good news, not of destruction and subjugation. How could the islanders have known of the Gospel before the missionaries came?"

Adeline clenched her fists, struggling to reconcile the teachings of her faith with the horrors she had just witnessed. She disapproved of colonialism and the subjugation that had followed. "This wasn't the way," she muttered, more to herself than to Nani. "This isn't what Papa wanted."

As if reading her thoughts, Nani nodded. "No, it wasn't. Papa's desire was for love, understanding, and respect. The Gospel was meant to be a message of hope and salvation, not a weapon of destruction."

Adeline's heart ached with the weight of this truth. She saw the faces of the islanders, their pain and confusion, their desperate struggle to hold on to their identity amidst the chaos.

"Look deeper, Adeline," Nani encouraged. "See beyond the actions of men to the heart of Papa's message."

Adeline closed her eyes, focusing on the teachings of Yeshua she had studied so diligently. She remembered the love, compassion, and mercy that Yeshua embodied. She saw Him reaching out to the marginalized, healing the sick, and embracing the lost with open arms. She saw His teachings of peace, love, and forgiveness. This was the essence of the Gospel—the good news meant to bring light and life, not pain and division.

In a vision, Adeline saw the Cook Islanders living in harmony with these true teachings. She saw them embracing the love of Yeshua without losing their cultural identity. She saw a blending of traditions, where the beauty of their heritage was celebrated alongside their new faith. She saw communities thriving in love and unity, without the scars of colonialism.

Adeline opened her eyes, her heart swelling with a renewed understanding. "Papa wanted the islanders to know His love, to find hope and salvation in His message, but without the loss of their own identity. They were meant to be disciples, not subjects of oppression."

Nani smiled, her eyes shining with approval. "Yes, Adeline. Papa's true desire is for harmony and peace, for all His children to live in love and unity."

Adeline took a deep breath, feeling the burden of her heritage and the responsibility it carried. She knew her journey was far from over. There were truths yet to be uncovered, battles yet to be fought, and hearts yet to be healed. As she looked out over the pristine waters of the Pacific, she felt a renewed sense of purpose.

The vision faded, and Adeline found herself back on the shore, the sun beginning to set. She felt a profound sense of connection to her ancestors and to the islanders who had suffered so much.

With Nani by her side, Adeline's resolve strengthened. She would honour her Celtic, Maori and Viking ancestry, but above all, she would honour the One who had created them all.

20

The Mountain of Questions

The mountain air was cool and crisp, a sharp contrast to the warm, tropical breezes of the Cook Islands. Adeline stood at the summit, gazing out over the rugged landscape of Scotland, with its rolling hills, craggy peaks, and mist-covered valleys. The beauty of the place was wild and untamed, a reflection of the land's ancient spirit. Yet, as she looked out over the horizon, her mind was filled with questions that had been stirring since her time in the islands.

Her journey had been extraordinary, a weaving together of the threads of her identity. In the Cook Islands, she had felt the deep connection to the earth, the ancestral wisdom of Nani and Te Ata Whetu, and the powerful presence of the ocean, which had taught her to embrace her identity and the sacredness of her Maori roots. But now, as she stood on Scottish soil, she felt a shift in the atmosphere, as if the land itself was preparing her for something important—something that would tie together all the strands of her journey.

Yeshua stood beside her, His presence as steady and comforting as ever. His gaze was fixed on the landscape, but Adeline knew that He was aware of the storm of thoughts swirling in her mind. She had so many questions, so many things she needed to understand, and she knew that now was the time to ask.

"Yeshua," she began, her voice hesitant but filled with determination, "I've been thinking a lot since I left Nani and Te Ata Whetu. I feel like everything I've learned is leading up to something important, but I still have so many questions about the past—about the history of our faith and how it's impacted so many lives."

Yeshua turned to her, His gaze gentle yet intense, inviting her to speak freely. "Ask, Addie. I'm here to listen and to help you understand."

She took a deep breath, gathering her thoughts. "In the Cook Islands, I felt such a strong connection to the land, to the stories of my ancestors. But now, being here in Scotland, I'm also feeling the weight of a different history—a history that isn't just about my Maori roots, but about the broader history of the Church. I've been reading about the Council of Nicaea, and how decisions were made that shaped the Bible and the faith we follow today. But there's so much I don't understand, especially about the role of Emperor Constantine and the brutal ways in which people were persecuted in the name of unifying different faiths under Christianity."

She paused, looking out over the rugged landscape, her heart heavy with the questions she had carried for so long. "How could something that started with You, with such pure intentions, lead to so much pain? How could the Church justify the exclusion of certain texts and the blending of pagan practices with the faith, all to accommodate political agendas?"

Yeshua's expression was filled with both sorrow and understanding. He walked a few steps ahead, and Adeline followed, the wind tugging at her hair as they moved closer to the edge of the mountain. From there, they could see the outline of ancient fortresses, and the remnants of battles fought long ago, their echoes still lingering in the air.

"Addie," Yeshua began, His voice soft but filled with authority, "the history of the Church is complex and layered, filled with moments of great faith and also great failure. The Council of Nicaea was a pivotal moment in history, where the early believers sought to protect and define the faith. They faced many challenges—heresies that threatened to distort the truth, and political pressures from leaders like Constantine, who sought to use Christianity as a tool to unify his empire."

He paused, His gaze scanning the horizon, His eyes reflecting a deep sadness. "In their efforts to create unity, they made decisions that would have lasting consequences. Some of those decisions were made out of fear—fear of division, fear of losing control. And in their zeal to protect what they believed was right, they excluded texts that they thought might lead people astray, but they also silenced voices that carried important truths."

Adeline's heart ached as she listened, but Yeshua's next words sent a chill down her spine. "Constantine's reign was not only marked by the blending of pagan practices with Christian faith, but also by a deliberate and brutal separation of Christianity from its Jewish roots. Constantine viewed the Jews with suspicion and contempt, seeing them as a threat to his vision of a unified Christian empire. Under his influence, laws were enacted that restricted Jewish practices, barred Jews from holding public office, and prohibited them from proselytizing. The Jewish people were increasingly marginalized, their connection to the early Church severed."

Yeshua's voice grew heavier as He continued. "The most devastating aspect of Constantine's policies was the violence that followed. In the name of solidifying the Christian faith, Jewish communities were targeted, persecuted, and often massacred. The very people through whom I came into the world were treated as enemies of the faith that was meant to be a fulfilment of their own covenant. This persecution laid the groundwork for centuries of suffering for the Jewish people, as Christianity, once deeply intertwined with Judaism, became increasingly hostile to its roots."

Adeline felt a deep sorrow wash over her. "But why, Yeshua? Why did this happen? How could the faith that was supposed to be about love and salvation lead to such darkness?"

Yeshua's eyes filled with compassion, His voice tinged with sorrow. "Constantine was a man of his time, influenced by the political and cultural forces around him. He saw the potential of Christianity to bring unity to his empire, but in doing so, he compromised the faith. He blended it with pagan practices, creating a version of Christianity that was more palatable to the masses but less true to its roots. And in his drive for unity, he allowed—and sometimes even encouraged—the persecution of those who did not conform, including the Jews."

He sighed, the weight of centuries of history seeming to rest upon His shoulders. "It grieves My heart deeply. The faith that I came to fulfil was meant to bring life, not death. It was meant to unite, not divide. But throughout history, My name has been used to justify terrible acts—acts that were the result of human sin, fear, and a misunderstanding of what it means to follow Me."

Adeline felt tears welling up in her eyes. "It's so hard to reconcile, Yeshua. To know that the faith I hold dear has also been used to cause so much pain. How do I move forward with this knowledge? How do I reconcile my faith in You with the history that's come before?"

Yeshua reached out, gently wiping away her tears. His touch was warm, comforting. "Addie, your faith in Me is not defined by the mistakes of the past. It is rooted in My love for you and the truth of who I am. The history of the Church is part of your inheritance, but it does not define your relationship with Me. You are called to live out your faith in a way that honours your heritage and the truth of My Word."

He looked deeply into her eyes, His voice filled with love and conviction. "The history you've learned is important. It's a reminder that even those who follow Me can fall into error, that the faith must be guarded carefully. But it's also a call to action. You, Addie, are part of the remnant—a voice for truth in a world that often forgets it. You are called to stand for justice, for righteousness, for the truth of My love. Let the knowledge of the past strengthen your resolve to live out the fullness of your faith, to embrace all that you are—Maori, Scottish, and a follower of Yeshua."

Adeline nodded, the weight of His words settling into her heart. She felt a deep sense of responsibility, but also a renewed sense of purpose. "I understand, Yeshua. It's not easy, but I know now that I'm called to stand in this place, to be a bridge between the past and the future. To hold onto the truth of who You are, even when the world around me seems to distort it."

Yeshua smiled, His expression filled with pride and love. "You are never alone, Addie. I am with you, always. And remember, the truth of My love is stronger than any darkness, any error, any division. It is the foundation upon which you stand, the light that will guide you through the days ahead."

As they stood together on the mountain, the wind began to pick up, swirling around them like a living thing. Adeline felt the ground beneath her shift slightly, and she knew that it was time to move on. She had spent time with Nani and Te Ata Whetu, learning the wisdom of her Maori ancestors, and now she was standing on the soil of Scotland, ready to embrace the next part of her journey.

Yeshua placed His hand gently on her shoulder. "The time has come, Addie. There are still many things for you to learn, many battles yet to be fought. But you are ready."

She nodded, her heart steady and her resolve firm. "I'm ready, Yeshua.

"Good," Yeshua replied, a spark of excitement in His eyes. "Papa is waiting for you."

Adeline felt a surge of anticipation as Yeshua's smile broadened. "I believe it's storytime!"

A thrill ran through her, knowing that each story Papa told held the keys to the mysteries she was unravelling. Adeline and Yeshua exchanged a grin, their eyes gleaming with the promise of what was to come.

"Let's not keep Him waiting," Adeline said, her voice filled with eagerness.

Together, they turned and began to walk, the atmosphere around them buzzing with the energy of the journey ahead. The path before them was filled with secrets waiting to be revealed, and Adeline could feel the pulse of history and destiny drawing her forward.

The next chapter of her adventure was about to begin.

21

The Norse Seafarers

Adeline, having immersed herself in the vibrant stories of her Polynesian heritage, was curious to explore another facet of her ancestry—the tales of her Viking roots. She approached Papa with a glint of excitement in her eyes, eager to unravel the history that lay hidden in the Norse sagas.

"Papa," she began, "tell me about our Viking ancestors. What stories do we have from that side of our family?"

Papa, with a knowing smile, welcomed Adeline's curiosity. "Ah, the Vikings! Your blood runs deep with the spirit of exploration, seafaring, and a warrior's heart. Let me share with you some tales that echo through the halls of your Norse lineage."

He began by recounting the saga of Erik the Red, a famed Viking explorer and father of Leif Erikson. "Erik the Red, your many times great-grandfather, was known for his adventurous spirit. Banished from Iceland, he sailed westward and discovered Greenland. There, he established the first Norse settlement, proving your Viking ancestors' resilience in harsh environments."

Adeline, captivated by the tale, envisioned the vast expanse of the North Atlantic as Erik the Red forged a new path for their family. "What happened next, Papa?"

Papa continued, "Erik's son, Leif Erikson, continued the legacy of exploration. Leif is often credited as one of the first Europeans to set foot in North America, around the 11th century—centuries before Columbus. He called the land Vinland, and your Viking ancestors left their mark on the shores of the New World."

Adeline marvelled at the thought of her ancestors navigating uncharted waters, their longships cutting through the waves of the North Atlantic. "It's incredible to think about the vast distances they travelled."

Papa nodded, "Indeed, their navigational skills rivalled those of any in their time. But it wasn't just about exploration; the Vikings were fierce warriors with a deep sense of honour and loyalty. There's a tale of your ancestor, Sigurd the Dragon Slayer, who defeated the mighty serpent Fafnir to claim a treasure. The story speaks of courage, cunning, and the triumph of good over evil."

Adeline, drawn into the world of Norse mythology, asked, "Tell me more about the gods and goddesses, Papa. What stories do we have about them?"

Papa smiled, "Ah, the pantheon of Norse gods and goddesses! Odin, the All-Father, the wise and powerful chief of the Aesir; Thor, the thunder god with his mighty hammer; Freyja, the goddess of love and fertility—these are just a few of the deities woven into your family's history. The Norse sagas are filled with their exploits, each reflecting aspects of our values and beliefs."

Adeline, with a thirst for knowledge, continued to delve into the tales of her Viking roots. As Papa began to recount the stories of the Norse gods and goddesses, a hearty laughter escaped his lips.

"Now, my dear Adeline," Papa chuckled, "these Norse gods, as fascinating as their stories may be, are clearly not the One True God you worship!" He winked at her, feigning shock and mockery. They both giggled at his antics. "They are but characters in the tapestry of your heritage, each with their own quirks and tales, combined with and huge dollop of ego and a tad of fabrication!"

Adeline, appreciating Papa's laughter and his gentle reminder of their family's faith, nodded in agreement. "Of course, Papa. I'm curious about our cultural history, but I always remember who's really on the throne!"

Papa's laughter echoed through the room, creating an atmosphere of warmth and understanding. "That's my clever daughter. Now, let me tell you about Odin. He was considered the chief of the Aesir, a wise and powerful figure. Some say he sacrificed an eye at the Well of Urd for wisdom. Quite the character, wouldn't you say?"

Adeline joined in the laughter, imagining Odin making such a sacrifice for knowledge. "And what about Thor, the thunder god?"

Papa, still chuckling, continued, "Ah, Thor and his mighty hammer, Mjolnir! He was the protector of mankind and defender against the forces of chaos. The stories speak of his adventures and battles, often accompanied by the sound of thunder."

As the tales unfolded, Papa's laughter became a joyful accompaniment to the stories of gods and goddesses. He shared the myth of Loki, the trickster, whose antics often led to humorous and unexpected consequences. Adeline found herself enthralled not only by the narratives but also by the infectious laughter that made the stories come to life.

Papa, sensing Adeline's genuine interest, shared more tales of their Viking ancestors, blending the richness of their cultural history with the lightness of laughter. The room echoed with stories of exploration, valour, and the occasional mischievousness of figures like Te Ruru.

As the night progressed, Adeline felt a profound connection to both her Polynesian and Viking heritages, appreciating the laughter that wove through the fabric of her family stories. In the shared moments of storytelling and laughter, she realized that her cultural history was not just a collection of tales but a living, breathing legacy that shaped her understanding of the world.

As the night unfolded, Adeline discovered the rich tapestry of her Viking heritage—the sagas of exploration, the feats of legendary warriors, and the myths that shaped the worldview of her Norse ancestors. She felt a deep connection to the resilience and adventurous spirit that flowed through both her Polynesian and Viking lineages, recognizing that each strand of her ancestry contributed to the vibrant mosaic of who she was.

As Adeline continued to explore the tales of her Viking heritage with Papa, the name Ragnar Lothbrok emerged like a legendary thread weaving through the stories of exploration and conquest. Papa, with a twinkle in his eye, decided to share a tale that echoed through the hills of Scotland.

"Adeline, let me tell you about Ragnar Lothbrok, a legendary figure among the Vikings. Ragnar was not only a skilled warrior but also a masterful tactician and explorer. Legend has it that he set foot in the lands of Scotland during his daring voyages."

Adeline's eyes widened with curiosity as Papa began to narrate the exploits of Ragnar Lothbrok. "Ragnar, driven by a spirit of adventure and a thirst for glory, led his warriors across the seas. They faced storms, treacherous waters, and, of course, encounters with rival clans. It's said that Ragnar and his crew made their way to the rugged shores of Scotland, seeking both conquest and new opportunities."

Papa, with a storyteller's flair, continued, "In the misty landscapes of Scotland, Ragnar and his warriors left their mark. They engaged in both fierce battles and trade, interacting with the local Picts and Gaels. Ragnar's presence, much like the fierce winds that swept across the Scottish hills, left a lasting impact on the region."

Adeline imagined the mighty longships arriving on the Scottish shores, the Norse warriors led by the enigmatic Ragnar Lothbrok. "What happened during their time in Scotland, Papa?"

Papa chuckled, "Ah, that's where the tales become a blend of history and legend. Some say Ragnar faced formidable foes; others claim he forged alliances with local leaders. The stories of his time in Scotland are as varied as the landscapes he encountered."

As they continued to discuss Ragnar Lothbrok's exploits, Adeline felt a connection to this legendary figure who, like her Polynesian ancestors, embodied the spirit of exploration and resilience. The stories of Ragnar's time in Scotland became another layer in the intricate tapestry of her heritage.

Papa, with a knowing smile, said, "Ragnar Lothbrok was a symbol of the Viking Age, a time of great voyages and bold endeavours. His legacy, much like the stories of Te Ruru and the tales from the Polynesian islands, is part of your family's adventurous spirit."

In the quiet of the evening, as they spoke of the Vikings and their journeys, Adeline couldn't help but marvel at the diverse stories that made up her ancestral history—stories that spanned continents and centuries, echoing the resilience, courage, and curiosity that defined her family's legacy. But as the last of the tales faded into the night, there in the shadows, she saw the tall, dark figure again—waiting. His presence lingered like a silent threat, a reminder that not all of her ancestral past was filled with light. She swallowed hard, knowing that eventually, she would have to face him.

22

The Gathering of Strength

Adeline's heart raced with a mix of excitement and apprehension as she neared the castle. The ancient fortress, perched high on a rugged hill, seemed to loom larger with every step she took. Its stone walls were weathered by centuries of wind and rain, standing as a testament to the battles fought and secrets kept within. The memories of her time in the islands, learning about her Polynesian heritage, were still fresh in her mind, but now she was returning to a place that connected her to a different part of her lineage—a place where her Viking roots and her present collided.

As she drew closer, the castle's heavy wooden doors creaked open, revealing the familiar faces she had longed to see. Drew, her Abba, stood at the entrance, his tall frame silhouetted against the warm glow of the firelight that spilled from within. His eyes lit up with a mix of joy and relief as he spotted Adeline. "Adeline, my girl," he said, his voice thick with emotion, as he pulled her into a strong embrace. "Welcome home."

Adeline melted into the comfort of his arms, feeling the weight of the months spent apart dissolve in the warmth of his welcome. "It's so good to be home, Abba," she whispered, her voice barely containing the tears that threatened to spill over.

Next, Alex, her Eema, stepped forward, her gentle smile radiating the love and tenderness that had been a constant in Adeline's life. She wrapped Adeline in a soft, motherly hug, the familiar scent of musk and vanilla instantly calming her. "We've missed you so much," Alex murmured, brushing a stray lock of hair from Adeline's face. "It hasn't been the same without you."

Before Adeline could respond, she was nearly bowled over by the exuberant hug of her younger brother, Davvie. "Adeline!" he shouted with boyish enthusiasm, squeezing her tightly. His energy was infectious, and Adeline couldn't help but laugh, her heart swelling with affection. "You've been gone forever!"

"I've missed you too, Davvie," Adeline said, ruffling his hair affectionately. "It's good to see you, little brother."

As she looked up, she caught sight of Claudine, her sister, standing nearby with a smile that was both warm and welcoming. Claudine's eyes glistened with unshed tears as she stepped forward and enveloped Adeline in a long, comforting hug. The embrace was filled with unspoken words, the kind that only sisters could share. "I'm so glad you're back, Addie," Claudine whispered, using the nickname she had given Adeline when they were children. "It's been too long."

Adeline held on tightly, drawing strength from the warmth and love that only Claudine could provide. "I've missed you, Claude," she replied, her voice thick with emotion. "It feels like I've been away for a lifetime."

Leo, Claudine's husband and their brother-in-law, stood close by, his expression a mix of welcome and gentle amusement at the sight of the two sisters reunited. When Claudine finally released Adeline, Leo stepped forward with a smile. "It's good to have you back, Addie," he said sincerely, offering a firm handshake that turned into a brief, brotherly hug. "We've been holding down the fort, but it's not the same without you."

The warmth of the reunion filled the courtyard, the ancient stones seeming to glow with the shared affection of the family. It was a moment of pure joy, but beneath the surface, there was an undercurrent of something more—something that weighed on each of them.

After the initial greetings, the family guided Adeline into the grand hall of the castle, where a fire crackled warmly in the hearth. The hall was as ancient as the castle itself, with high, vaulted ceilings and walls adorned with tapestries that depicted scenes from battles long past. As they settled into the old wooden chairs around a long table, the mood gradually shifted from the joy of reunion to a more serious tone. The firelight flickered, casting shadows that danced across the stone walls, as if echoing the weight of the conversation that was about to unfold.

Mirabelle, the steadfast leader of their group, took a seat across from Adeline, her expression serious but tinged with the warmth that had been so evident during their reunion. "Adeline, there's much we need to discuss," she began, her voice carrying the weight of the past few months. "While you were away, we spent time in Qumran. We uncovered ancient texts and prophecies that have deep implications for all of us—especially for you."

Adeline's attention sharpened, her heart pounding as she sensed the gravity of what Mirabelle was about to reveal. Papa, ever the wise and calming presence, continued the explanation. "The texts we found spoke of a great spiritual battle that is tied to our Viking ancestry. The place we're in now, this castle, is more than just a historical site. It's a nexus, a place where our past and future intersect."

The words hung in the air, heavy with significance. Adeline's mind raced as she tried to piece together the implications of what they were saying. "What does this mean for us?" she asked, her voice steady but tinged with concern.

Alex, her Eema, leaned forward, her expression filled with both love and the seriousness of the situation. "It means that the forces of darkness tied to our ancestors have been awakened. We're here because this is where the battle will begin, and it's a battle we must be prepared to fight—not just with our physical strength but with our faith."

Davvie, ever the inquisitive younger brother, added, "We found evidence that this place has been a battleground before, during the times of our Viking ancestors. The spirits that were left behind... they're restless, and they're looking for something —or someone."

A chill ran down Adeline's spine as she absorbed their words. The gravity of the situation became clear, the way it hung in the air like a storm waiting to break. "How do we prepare for this?" she asked, her voice calm but resolute.

Mirabelle's eyes met hers with a steady gaze. "You've been preparing for this all along, Adeline. Your time in the islands, learning about your Polynesian heritage, was not just about connecting with your past. It was also about strengthening your spirit, about understanding who you are and the power that comes from that knowledge."

Petrucia, their foremother, who had been silently observing the exchange, now stepped forward. Her presence was commanding yet filled with a quiet grace that seemed to emanate from within. "Adeline, you are stronger than you know. The battles we face are not just of flesh and blood but against spiritual forces. We must arm ourselves with prayer, with the Word of God, and with the unwavering faith that Yeshua will guide us through."

Adeline nodded, feeling the weight of her foremother's words settle into her heart. She knew that her journey was far from over and that the real challenge was just beginning. "I've never fought a battle like this before," she admitted, looking around at the faces of those she loved.

At that moment, Jeanne d'Arc, the fierce and faithful warrior, stepped forward. Her eyes met Adeline's with a look of determination that was both encouraging and resolute. "Then it's time you learned," she said, her voice firm yet kind. "I will train you, Adeline. You have the heart of a warrior, but now you must learn to wield the sword with skill and confidence."

Jeanne led Adeline out into the courtyard, where the storm clouds gathered ominously overhead. The wind picked up, swirling the leaves and carrying with it the scent of rain. The atmosphere crackled with anticipation, a reflection of the tension that lay within Adeline's heart.

Jeanne unsheathed her sword, the blade catching the light as it cut through the air. "This isn't just about learning to fight," she said, her tone serious. "It's about understanding the power that comes from within—the power that is given to you by Yeshua. You must fight with your faith as much as with your sword."

Adeline, gripping the hilt of her own sword, nodded. She felt a deep sense of readiness mixed with the nerves of someone about to face the unknown. Jeanne began with the basics, guiding her through the stances and movements that would make her strong and agile. With each swing, Adeline felt herself growing more confident, her earlier doubts being slowly replaced with a sense of purpose.

As they trained, Jeanne shared stories of her own battles, how she had relied on her faith and the guidance of Yeshua to overcome overwhelming odds. "Remember, Adeline," Jeanne said as she demonstrated a defensive move, "your strength comes from your faith. Never forget that the Lord is your shield, and with Him, you can overcome any foe."

The hours passed quickly, the storm clouds inching ever closer as the sky darkened. By the time they finished, Adeline felt a newfound confidence. She was exhausted, but it was the satisfying weariness that came from being pushed to grow.

As they returned to the grand hall, the first drops of rain began to fall, pattering against the stone walls of the castle. The family gathered once more, their faces reflecting a shared understanding of the challenge that lay ahead. They had been brought together for a purpose, and now, with Adeline prepared and the knowledge they had gained from Qumran, they were ready to face whatever awaited them.

In the stillness that followed, Adeline offered a prayer, her voice strong and clear. "Yeshua, guide us in the battles to come. Strengthen our hands and our hearts, and lead us in Your truth. We place our trust in You, knowing that with Your light, we can face any darkness."

As her words faded, a profound sense of peace settled over the group. The tension in the room seemed to dissolve, replaced by a quiet but unshakable resolve. The storm outside continued to gather strength, the wind howling as it whipped around the castle walls, but inside, the family was united, ready to face whatever challenges lay ahead.

Papa appeared, his expression one of quiet determination. "You've been brought here for a reason," he said, his voice steady. "This castle holds more than just the echoes of your past —it's where your destiny will unfold. You are here to confront the forces that have haunted your family for generations, and with Yeshua as your guide, you will prevail."

Adeline looked around the room, taking in the faces of those she loved. Her family, her allies, her strength. The bond they shared was unbreakable, forged not just by blood but by the trials they had faced together and the faith that anchored them. They were ready.

As the family prepared to settle in for the night, the atmosphere in the castle shifted. The walls, once seeming to close in with the weight of their history, now felt like a fortress of protection, a place where they could stand together and face the coming storm. They knew that the battle would not be easy, but they were not alone. They had each other, and they had their faith.

Adeline walked to the window, looking out over the darkened landscape. The storm clouds hung low, heavy with rain and thunder, but she no longer felt the fear that had gripped her earlier. Instead, she felt a deep sense of purpose, a calling that resonated in her very soul. She was where she needed to be, surrounded by those who would fight alongside her, ready to uncover the secrets of this ancient place and to confront whatever darkness lay in wait.

Claudine joined her at the window, slipping an arm around her shoulders in a gesture of sisterly solidarity. "Whatever comes, Addie, we'll face it together," she said softly.

Adeline smiled, leaning into the warmth of her sister's embrace. "Together," she echoed, feeling the truth of the word settle into her heart.

The castle, with its ancient stones and weathered battlements, stood as a silent witness to the gathering storm. But within its walls, the family gathered, their faith and love for one another a beacon of light in the encroaching darkness. The battle was coming, and they would be ready.

As the first drops of rain began to fall, the family prepared for the night ahead, each drawing strength from the shared moments of prayer and the deep connections that bound them. They were not just fighting for their own survival, but for the legacy of those who had come before them, and for the future of those who would come after. And with Yeshua guiding them, they knew that, no matter what, they would stand victorious.

The storm outside raged on, but inside the castle, peace reigned. The battle was imminent, but so was the victory that their faith promised. They were ready, and with that thought, Adeline and her family settled into the night, prepared for whatever the dawn might bring.

23

The Call to Arms

The stormy night left little sense of refreshment as the family arose the next morning. To their surprise, there was a beautiful breakfast laid out for them on the long table they had convened at the previous night.

With a crack that shook the ancient windows, the group were startled and felt the surge of storm directly upon them. It was time to walk through the castle and go where Ruah (Holy Spirit) was leading them. As they walked through the building, they were amazed at the former opulence and grandeur of its contents. Walking past large rooms, long hallways, beautiful bedrooms and stunning vistas out the windows, the air felt dark and foreboding.

The group's exploration led them to a grand, yet ominous, library filled with ancient tomes and scrolls. The room was vast, its high ceilings and towering bookshelves giving it an almost cathedral-like quality. The air was thick with the scent of aged paper and dust, and a heavy silence hung over the space, as if the very walls were holding their breath. Claudine, attuned to the spiritual realm, felt a strange pull toward one particular section of the library. She paused, her brow furrowing as she tried to make sense of the sensation. It was as though something in the castle was calling to her, something hidden within these walls, something that did not wish to be found.

Claudine's steps slowed as she approached a large, dusty shelf filled with ancient manuscripts. She ran her fingers lightly over the spines of the books, her gaze unfocused, following the inexplicable tug in her spirit. The others noticed her change in demeanour and fell silent, watching her with a mixture of curiosity and concern. Finally, she stopped in front of a large, ornate bookshelf that seemed slightly out of place among the others.

"Something's here," Claudine murmured, more to herself than to the others. She glanced at Davvie, her younger brother, who had a natural curiosity and a knack for noticing the unusual. "Can you feel it?"

Davvie nodded, stepping forward. "Yeah… it's like the air is heavier here."

Following Claudine's intuition, Davvie examined the stone wall behind the shelves. His fingers traced the cold, uneven surface, searching for anything that felt out of place. The stones were rough under his touch, ancient and worn, but as his hand moved across the wall, he suddenly felt something different. His fingers found a loose stone, slightly protruding from the wall. With a slight push, the stone shifted, and a faint grinding sound echoed through the silent library.

The group exchanged glances, their unease growing. Slowly, the bookshelf began to move, sliding aside to reveal a hidden passageway. The darkness beyond the entrance was thick and impenetrable, and a draft of cold air seeped out, chilling them to the bone. Whatever lay beyond this passage, they knew it held the answers they sought—or perhaps something far more dangerous.

Steeling themselves, the group stepped into the narrow passage, the walls closing in around them as they moved deeper into the bowels of the castle. The air grew colder with each step, and a sense of foreboding gripped them all. The flickering light from their torches barely penetrated the darkness, casting long, eerie shadows that seemed to dance on the walls. The passage twisted and turned, leading them further away from the library and into the unknown depths of the castle.

Finally, the passage opened into a small chamber, untouched for centuries. The room was lit by a single, ethereal light source that seemed to have no visible origin, casting an otherworldly glow on the ancient stones. The walls were lined with runes and symbols, remnants of ancient Viking rituals. The markings were old, their meanings lost to time, but their presence filled the room with an energy that was heavy, almost malevolent. It was as if the very air was thick with the spirits of those who had once inhabited this place.

In the centre of the room stood a stone pedestal, upon which rested a large, weathered tome bound in dark leather. The group hesitated at the threshold, sensing the powerful, unsettling energy that radiated from the book. But Adeline, feeling an overwhelming sense of purpose, stepped forward. Her heart pounded in her chest as she approached the pedestal, the pull of the tome irresistible.

With trembling hands, she opened the book. The pages were filled with intricate drawings and writings in a language long forgotten by the living. As Adeline began to read, the words seemed to resonate within the very walls of the chamber. The group huddled closer, drawn into the dark history that began to unfold before them.

The tome revealed the story of Erik Bloodbane, a Viking chieftain who had made a pact with demonic forces—an unholy alliance forged in blood to grant him power and dominion in life and death. The ritual described in the tome bound the spirits of his vanquished enemies to his will, turning them into his spectral army. These spirits, cursed and restless, had remained trapped within the castle's walls for centuries, and now, awakened by the group's presence, they were stirring once more.

As Adeline read aloud from the tome, the temperature in the room plummeted. A low, guttural whisper echoed through the chamber, the voice speaking in a tongue that none of them could fully comprehend. The walls seemed to close in, and a wave of dread washed over them all. The realization hit them like a blow—they had unwittingly activated the ancient curse, triggering the manifestation of the spectral Viking spirits bound to Erik Bloodbane.

Suddenly, the room began to shake, and the light source dimmed, casting long, menacing shadows. Claudine's visions flooded her mind with images of the battles fought by Erik Bloodbane and his spectral army. She saw the faces of those who had perished in those long-ago battles, their souls still trapped in the castle's walls, crying out for release.

The ground beneath them trembled as the walls seemed to pulse with a dark energy. The atmosphere grew thicker, almost suffocating, as if the very castle was reacting to the curse being unleashed. Adeline's hands tightened around the tome as she struggled to comprehend the magnitude of what they had discovered.

As the tremors intensified, a hidden compartment beneath the stone pedestal suddenly opened with a loud click, revealing a small, intricately carved box. Inside the box was a fragment of an ancient artifact—a piece of a weapon or relic tied to the family's lineage. The artifact glowed faintly, its significance immediately apparent to everyone in the room. This relic, when combined with the family's celestial connection, could be the key to breaking the curse and defeating Erik Bloodbane once and for all.

But before they could fully grasp the significance of their discovery, the room was plunged into darkness, and a chilling wind swept through the chamber. The ominous energy they had sensed earlier now felt almost tangible, pressing down on them with a malevolent force.

The group, now fully aware of the danger they had awakened, raced out of the secret chamber, knowing they had little time to prepare for what was to come. As they emerged back into the library, the castle itself seemed to come alive. The walls echoed with distant sounds—battle cries, the clashing of swords, and the mournful wails of spirits long departed. The spectral Viking spirits had awakened, and the Army was about to be thrust into a battle unlike any they had faced before.

As they gathered their wits, the realization dawned on them that the battle Erik Bloodbane had sought to continue through the centuries was now at hand. The curse had been unleashed, and the castle that had stood as a silent witness to history's darkest moments would once again become a battlefield. The group exchanged determined glances, knowing that they were not only fighting for their lives but for the souls of those bound to the castle's dark past. The time for preparation was over—the battle had begun.

The storm raged outside, its fury a physical manifestation of the battle that was about to unfold. Lightning cracked across the darkened sky, illuminating the ancient castle walls in brief, blinding flashes. Thunder rolled like a war drum, shaking the very ground beneath their feet as the Army stepped out into the courtyard, weapons in hand, ready to face the spectral Viking spirits that had been awakened.

The air was thick with anticipation, the howling wind carrying with it the cries of the restless dead. The storm was no ordinary tempest—it was a living, breathing entity, a reflection of the chaos and darkness that Erik Bloodbane and his demonic forces had unleashed upon the world. The clouds churned above, black and ominous, swirling like a vortex of evil.

Adeline stood at the forefront, her sword gripped tightly in her hand. The blade, a gift from Mirabelle, glowed faintly with a celestial light, its power a beacon of hope amidst the darkness. Beside her were Claudine, Mirabelle, Jeanne d'Arc, and the rest of the Army, their faces set with determination and resolve. This was the battle they had been preparing for, the moment when their faith would be tested against the forces of evil.

As the Army took their positions in the courtyard, the ground beneath them began to tremble once more. The stones of the castle seemed to groan under the weight of the spiritual forces at play, and from the shadows, the spectral Viking spirits began to emerge. Their forms were twisted and grotesque, eyes glowing with a malevolent light. They were clad in ancient armor, their weapons forged not of steel, but of darkness itself.

At the head of the spectral army stood Erik Bloodbane, his presence overwhelming. His eyes burned with a deep, otherworldly fire, and his armour was etched with runes of power and death. In his hand, he held a massive axe, its blade dripping with the essence of the damned. His voice, when he spoke, was a guttural growl that seemed to echo from the depths of the abyss.

"Fools," Erik sneered, his voice cutting through the howling wind. "You dare to challenge me? You dare to think you can undo the curse that has bound me for centuries?"

Adeline stepped forward, her voice steady despite the fear that gnawed at her insides. "We do not fight with our own strength, Erik Bloodbane. We fight with the power of Yeshua, and His light will cast down your darkness."

Erik's laughter was a chilling sound, devoid of any trace of humanity. "Then let us see if your light can stand against the might of the damned."

With that, Erik raised his axe high, and the spectral army surged forward, their forms coalescing into a tide of shadow and flame. The storm above responded in kind, the wind whipping into a frenzy, and the rain beginning to fall in sheets, as if the heavens themselves were weeping for the battle about to take place.

The Army met the charge with a battle cry that pierced the storm, their voices rising above the chaos. Jeanne d'Arc, her armour gleaming even in the dim light, led the first strike, her sword clashing with the spectral weapons of the Viking spirits. Her movements were fluid and precise, each strike a testament to her skill and divine purpose. Around her, the other members of the Army fought with equal fervour, their weapons glowing with the light of Yeshua.

Adeline found herself in the thick of the battle, her sword clashing against the ethereal weapons of the spirits. Each strike sent a shockwave of energy through the air, the impact of good against evil creating a tangible force that rippled through the courtyard. The storm above intensified, the lightning flashing so frequently that it was as if the battle were being fought under a strobe light.

Claudine, fighting nearby, wielded her weapon with calm precision, her every move guided by the visions that had been gifted to her. She saw not just the physical forms of the spirits but the threads of darkness that connected them to Erik Bloodbane. With each strike, she aimed not just to defeat her enemies but to sever the ties that bound them to the chieftain's will.

Mirabelle, adorned in her deep burgundy armour, moved with an ethereal grace, her bow in hand. Each arrow she loosed was infused with the power of intuition and guidance, striking true against the spectral foes. Her presence was a calming force in the chaos, her leadership a beacon that kept the Army focused and strong.

As the battle raged on, the storm seemed to reach a crescendo. The wind howled like a living beast, the rain drove down in torrents, and the thunder boomed like the footsteps of giants. The darkness pressed in from all sides, but the Army fought on, their faith shining like a beacon in the night.

Erik Bloodbane, seeing his forces begin to falter against the might of the Army, let out a roar of rage. His eyes blazed as he charged forward, his massive axe swinging with a force that could cleave the very earth. He moved with a speed and power that defied his spectral form, his attacks relentless.

Adeline met his charge, her heart pounding in her chest as their weapons clashed. The impact sent a shockwave through the courtyard, the force of it driving her back a step. Erik's strength was overwhelming, his power born of centuries of hatred and darkness. But Adeline did not waver. She called upon the strength of Yeshua, her faith a shield against the darkness that threatened to consume her.

With each strike, she felt the light within her grow stronger, pushing back against the malevolent force of Erik Bloodbane. Around her, the Army fought with renewed vigour, their voices lifting in prayer and praise as they battled the demonic forces.

The storm above seemed to reflect the intensity of the battle below. The wind reached a fevered pitch, the rain falling so heavily that it was difficult to see more than a few feet ahead. But even as the darkness pressed in, the light of Yeshua shone through, a force that could not be extinguished.

Finally, as the battle reached its peak, Adeline found herself standing face to face with Erik Bloodbane. His eyes blazed with hatred, his form flickering like a candle in the wind. "You cannot defeat me," he snarled, his voice a guttural growl. "I am eternal. I am darkness incarnate."

Adeline met his gaze, her sword held steady in her hand. "You may be darkness, but I carry the light of Yeshua within me. And that light will always prevail."

With a final, powerful strike, Adeline brought her sword down, the blade glowing with divine energy. The impact was like a bolt of lightning, piercing through the very essence of Erik Bloodbane. A scream of rage and despair echoed through the courtyard as the chieftain's form began to dissolve, the darkness that had held him together unravelling.

As Erik Bloodbane was cast down, the storm above suddenly ceased. The wind died away, the rain stopped, and the dark clouds that had hung so heavily over the castle began to part. Rays of sunlight broke through, flooding the courtyard with a warm, golden light. The spectral army, now leaderless, began to fade, their forms dissolving into the air like mist in the morning sun.

The Army stood victorious, their breaths coming in ragged gasps as they surveyed the battlefield. The storm that had raged so fiercely was gone, replaced by the bright, clear light of day. The sun, now fully visible in the sky, shone down upon them, a symbol of the victory they had achieved.

Adeline lowered her sword, the weight of what they had accomplished settling over her. The battle was over, the darkness vanquished. She looked around at her family and allies, their faces lit by the warm sunlight, and felt a deep sense of peace. They had faced the darkness, and they had won.

As the last remnants of the storm cleared, the castle courtyard was transformed. The stones, once cold and foreboding, now seemed to glow in the sunlight, the shadows that had clung to them banished by the light. The curse that had held the castle in its grip for centuries was broken, and with it, the spirits of those who had been bound to Erik Bloodbane were finally at rest.

The family gathered together in the centre of the courtyard, their faces turned toward the sun. They had fought a great battle, but they had not fought alone. Yeshua had been with them every step of the way, guiding their hands, strengthening their hearts, and leading them to victory.

In the silence that followed, Adeline offered a final prayer of thanks, her voice carried on the gentle breeze that now whispered through the courtyard. "Thank you, Yeshua, for guiding us, for protecting us, and for leading us to victory. We place our future in Your hands, knowing that with You, we can face anything."

The battle was over, but their journey was far from finished. Together, they turned and walked inside, heading back to the secret room.

24

Unearthed Memories

The hidden chamber, bathed in an ethereal glow, seemed to carry the weight of ages. Petrucia, Jeanne, and Moshe, their presence warm and strong, gestured toward the artefacts that filled the room. The group hadn't noticed them before and were genuinely surprised by the relics. Each item held a story—pieces of the family's seafaring past, connecting them to different lands and times.

As Adeline carefully turned the pages of an ancient tome, a sudden breeze seemed to stir the pages, revealing more than just Viking seafaring exploits. It also uncovered connections with Polynesian voyagers, a tapestry of journeys that stretched from the Cook Islands to the shores of Scotland. Adeline's eyes widened in amazement as she studied the maps. The routes traced across the parchment revealed intricate paths linking distant places, weaving together the cultures of Polynesia and Scotland.

Petrucia, Jeanne, and Moshe looked on as Adeline absorbed this revelation, confirming the connections between the family's diverse roots. Jeanne and Moshe's gentle nods reinforced what she was discovering, but it was Petrucia who stepped closer, her face filled with pride and a hint of emotion.

"There were many moments," Petrucia began softly, "when I wanted to tell you, Adeline. About these connections, these journeys. But I was bound by Papa's confidence in you. He trusted that you would discover these truths in your own way, in your own time. And now, you have."

Adeline looked up at her foremother, feeling a mix of gratitude and awe. "You knew all along?" she asked, her voice filled with emotion.

Petrucia smiled warmly, placing a hand on Adeline's shoulder. "Yes. And I am so proud of you. This isn't just about your heritage—it's about your courage, your strength, and your heart. You were meant to find this."

Adeline's heart swelled with pride, the full weight of her lineage settling within her. These maps and artefacts were not just historical records—they were a living testament to the resilience and unity of her ancestors, showing how far they had travelled and how deeply they were connected across the oceans.

As the group continued exploring the room, Claudine, with her keen insight, began interpreting sketches and writings from the ancient tome. These revealed not only the dark history of Erik Bloodbane but also the strength of the noble clan that had stood against him. The artefacts were more than relics—they were markers of the clan's courage and the celestial guidance they had received.

Drew, Leo, and Davvie immersed themselves in the objects scattered throughout the room. Each piece spoke of their family's deep seafaring roots. Leo, studying an old compass that still pointed north, uncovered coded messages hidden within the maps, revealing stories of cooperation and the celestial forces that had steered their ancestors. Davvie, examining a meticulously crafted model of a Viking longship, felt the connection to his Celtic, Viking, and Polynesian heritage stirring within him.

Then, as if summoned by the weight of the revelations, Erik Bloodbane's spirit appeared before them. His presence, though powerful, was no longer menacing. Erik had been changed by the celestial battle they had fought. His once dark and vengeful form now carried an air of calm and reflection. His eyes landed on Adeline, and for a moment, they were filled with something close to admiration.

"You've grown into a strong warrior, Adeline," Erik said, his voice carrying the respect of a seasoned fighter. "You've faced darkness head-on, and you've won—not just with a sword, but with courage and light."

Adeline stood tall, meeting his gaze. She had seen him in his darkest moments, but now there was something different in his tone.

Erik's spirit began to recount his life—how his ambition had led him down a dark path of conquest and power. He spoke of his rise as a Viking chieftain, his conquests, and how he had come into conflict with a noble Scottish clan. This clan, he explained, had been guided by the very celestial forces that now surrounded Adeline and her family—Petrucia, Jeanne, and Moshe.

"The noble clan fought against me," Erik said, his voice carrying the weight of regret. "And they had something I didn't understand at the time—faith. They were never alone. Even when I pushed them to the edge, they were protected by forces greater than anything I could summon."

The family listened intently as Erik's story unfolded—a tale of ambition, battles, and a slow realization that power alone could not bring peace. The clan had been able to resist him not just through strength, but through their trust in the divine.

Adeline stepped forward, her voice steady. "You've seen both sides now—darkness and light. What do you want us to take from your story?"

Erik paused, his gaze sweeping the room. "My story is a warning, and a lesson. Ambition without purpose leads to ruin. But you, Adeline, have something I never had. You understand the power of faith and unity. And that's why you were able to defeat me."

His form flickered slightly, but there was no anger or malice —only acceptance. "I fought against the wrong things. Now, I see that strength comes not from domination, but from courage, from faith, and from standing together."

The room, filled with the echoes of Erik's words, became a space for reflection. The family, standing among the artefacts and maps, now understood their deeper connection to the past— how their ancestors, with the guidance of Petrucia, Jeanne, and Moshe, had stood strong against darkness. And how that same strength flowed through them now.

Petrucia, watching Adeline closely, nodded with a quiet smile. "You are ready," she whispered. "Your journey has only just begun."

As Erik's spirit began to fade, the weight of the curse that had bound him for centuries finally lifted. The dark hold that had chained his soul was shattered, not by force of arms, but by the light of Yeshua working through Adeline and the family. It was their faith, their trust in God's strength, that had allowed the curse to be broken. No longer a slave to his past, Erik's spirit found peace.

Before he disappeared completely, Erik looked at them one last time. "The curse is broken because you did not rely on your own strength," he said quietly, his voice filled with a mixture of gratitude and awe. "You fought with the power of God, and that is why you were victorious."

The room seemed to exhale in relief, the heavy atmosphere lifting. As the presence of the curse dissolved, a sense of peace and divine presence filled the space. The family stood united, knowing that they had not fought alone. They had been instruments of God's will, their victory a testament to the power of faith, unity, and the guidance of Yeshua.

Petrucia, her eyes filled with love and pride, spoke softly. "The battle is won, and the curse is gone. But remember, it was never by your might or by your own power. It was by the Spirit of God working through you."

And with that, the room, once a place of dark secrets, became a sanctuary of light and renewed purpose—a reminder that with God, even the deepest darkness can be overcome.

25

Threads of Destiny

The sun was beginning to dip below the horizon, casting long shadows across the ancient stones of the fortress. Adeline stood at the edge of the crumbling walls, looking out over the vast expanse of desert that stretched as far as the eye could see. The air was still and heavy with the heat of the day, but there was a coolness coming in with the evening breeze, a relief from the relentless sun.

She had always felt a connection to this place, but now, after everything she had learned, that connection felt deeper, more profound. The desert, with its stark beauty and harshness, had been the backdrop for so many of her recent adventures. She had always wondered why she was drawn to these places, why the sands seemed to call to her, why she felt at home in the wild landscapes of Scotland and the serene beauty of the islands. But now, it was all beginning to make sense.

Adeline had recently received the results of her DNA test. The news had been surprising, even shocking at first. She had discovered that she had Jewish ancestry—something she had never known, never even suspected. And not only that, but her grandfather's DNA showed a significant connection to the Middle East. It was as if her very blood had been speaking to her all along, leading her to these places, to these moments.

Papa stood beside her, His presence warm and reassuring. He had been quiet as she processed this new information, giving her the space she needed to understand it in her own time. But now, as the sun dipped lower and the sky began to blush with the colours of twilight, He knew it was time to speak.

"You've discovered much about yourself, Addie," He said softly, His voice carrying the weight of eternity yet as gentle as the breeze that stirred her hair. "You are beginning to see the threads that have woven together to form the tapestry of who you are."

Adeline nodded, still gazing out at the desert. "I never expected this, Papa. I never imagined that I had Jewish ancestry, or that Poppa's roots were so deeply connected to the Middle East. It's like… everything is shifting inside me. My identity, my faith… everything feels different now."

Papa's gaze was tender, filled with understanding. "The discovery of your heritage does not change who you are, Addie. It reveals more of who you have always been. Your journey through the desert, your experiences in Scotland and the islands —these were not just random adventures. They were part of My plan to show you who you are, to prepare you for what lies ahead."

Adeline turned to look at Him, her eyes searching His face for answers. "But why, Papa? Why does this matter so much now? Why do I need to know this, especially with everything that's happening in the world?"

Papa's eyes held hers, His expression both loving and solemn. "Because, My dear one, you are being called to stand in a time of great importance. The world is changing, and the forces of darkness are gathering strength. Your Jewish heritage, your connection to the land of Israel, and your faith in Yeshua—they are all part of the foundation you must stand on. You are called to be a light in this darkening world, to bear witness to the truth of who I am and what I have done."

Adeline felt a shiver run through her, a mix of awe and fear. "But I don't know if I'm ready for that, Papa. I don't know if I can do what You're asking of me."

Papa's hand rested gently on her shoulder, His touch grounding her in the moment. "You are ready, Addie. You have been prepared for this your entire life. The revelation of your heritage is not a burden, but a gift. It connects you to a story that is far greater than yourself, a story that began long before you were born and will continue long after you are gone."

She took a deep breath, letting His words sink in. "And what about my faith in Yeshua? How does this change that?"

Papa smiled, His expression filled with deep love. "Your faith in Yeshua is the cornerstone of everything. He is the fulfilment of the covenant I made with Israel, the promise of redemption for all who believe. Your heritage does not change that; it deepens it. You are part of the remnant, those who know the truth and are called to share it with the world. Your faith in Yeshua is what will give you the strength to stand, even when the world around you is falling apart."

Adeline felt tears prick at the corners of her eyes, overwhelmed by the weight of what she was hearing. "So, all of this—my DNA, my heritage, my faith—it's all connected?"

"Yes, Addie," Papa said softly. "It is all connected. You are being called to stand in the gap, to be a voice for truth and a beacon of hope. The sands of the desert, the wildness of Scotland, the beauty of the islands—they have all been part of your journey to this moment. Now you must take hold of all these strands and weave them together into the person you are meant to be."

Adeline nodded, a sense of resolve settling over her. She knew what she had to do, even if it scared her. She was part of a greater story, one that was still being written. And she was ready to play her part.

"Thank you, Papa," she whispered, her voice steady despite the emotions swirling inside her. "I'll do what You've asked. I'll stand for what is true, for who I am, and for Yeshua."

Papa's smile was warm, filled with pride and love. "I know you will, my dear one. And remember, I am always with you."

As the last rays of sunlight faded from the sky, Adeline felt a sense of peace settle over her. The fortress, with its ancient stones and echoes of history, seemed to hold her in a gentle embrace, a reminder that she was never alone.

And then, as if in response to her newfound resolve, the ground beneath her feet began to shift. The stones of the fortress seemed to move, revealing an opening, a hidden passage that led deep into the earth. Adeline looked at Papa, who nodded encouragingly.

"It is time, Addie. The tunnels of Qumran await."

With one last look at the fortress, Adeline stepped into the opening, the cool air of the tunnels brushing against her skin. As she descended into the darkness, she felt a strange mix of fear and excitement. But she knew, deep in her heart, that she was exactly where she was meant to be. The journey was far from over, and the greatest revelations were yet to come.

26

Addie and Papa

Adeline adjusted her pack as she followed Papa through the winding tunnels of the subterranean city. The dim light of the torches illuminated their path, casting long shadows that flickered like whispers on the ancient stone walls. She marvelled at the craftsmanship of the ancient builders—how the stones seemed to fit together seamlessly, creating a labyrinth of secrets hidden from the world above.

Papa walked ahead with an ease that belied His age, if such a concept could even apply to Him. He moved with a timeless grace, the very essence of life and creation flowing through every step. Adeline couldn't help but smile as she watched Him, her heart swelling with affection and awe.

As they rounded a corner, Papa glanced back at her, His eyes twinkling with mischief. "You're not slowing down on me, are you, Addie?"

Adeline laughed, quickening her pace to catch up. "You know, for someone who's been around since the beginning of time, you sure can move fast!"

He chuckled, the sound like a melody that filled the space around them. "Well, I've had plenty of time to practice."

They shared a smile, the kind that spoke of deep understanding and shared history. It was a smile that reminded Adeline of just how blessed she was to have this time with Him—time that was both precious and rare.

As they continued their journey, the air grew cooler, the scent of earth and stone filling their lungs. They walked in comfortable silence for a while, the sound of their footsteps echoing softly in the tunnel.

Finally, they arrived at their destination—the small, dimly lit chamber tucked away within the subterranean city, the one they had been shown earlier. The room was small and covered with frescoes, with the large stone table in the centre, its surface covered in ancient tools and parchment. Addie hadn't noticed the walls were lined with shelves, each one filled with scrolls of varying sizes, their brittle edges peeking out from the shadows.

Adeline's breath caught in her throat as she took in the sight. She had seen many incredible things in her life, but there was something about this place that felt different—something sacred.

Papa watched her with a gentle smile, knowing the thoughts that swirled in her mind. "This is a place of great significance, Addie. It has been preserved for a reason. As you know, this is where the Sicarii and the Seraphimites gathered to work together, plan and pray."

Adeline stepped forward, her fingers grazing the edge of the stone table. The surface was cool to the touch, worn smooth by the passage of time. She felt a sense of reverence as she looked at the tools and parchment, each one a relic of a time long past.

"What were these used for?" she asked, her voice barely above a whisper.

Papa stepped beside her, His gaze thoughtful as He looked at the artifacts. "These tools were used by the scribes and artisans who lived here long ago, the Seraphimites, and some of the Sicarii too. They were the keepers of knowledge, the ones who recorded the words and wisdom that would be passed down through generations."

Adeline's eyes moved to the shelves lined with scrolls. "And these scrolls... what do they contain?"

Papa's smile widened, a spark of excitement in His eyes. "Oh, these scrolls hold treasures beyond measure. The words of Isaiah, Jeremiah, the minor prophets, and many others. Wisdom and prophecy, guidance and truth—all preserved here, waiting to be discovered."

Adeline's heart raced as she took in the magnitude of what she was seeing.

Papa's expression grew more serious, though there was still a warmth in His gaze. "They were hidden here by those who knew the value of these words. They understood that there would come a time when these truths would be desperately needed."

Adeline nodded, understanding the weight of His words. She knew that their journey had brought them here for a reason, but she couldn't help but feel a sense of wonder and excitement at the discovery.

She reached out and picked up one of the scrolls, handling it with care. The parchment was fragile; the ink faded with time, but the words were still legible. She unrolled it slightly, her eyes scanning the ancient script.

"Isaiah," she murmured, recognizing the familiar verses. "This is... incredible."

Papa watched her with a smile, His eyes filled with affection. "It is, isn't it? These words have been preserved for a reason, Addie. They're part of a greater plan."

Adeline looked up at Him, her brow furrowing slightly. "What plan?"

Papa's expression softened, and He reached out to gently take the scroll from her hands, rolling it back up with practised ease. "There's something I need to share with you, Addie. It's important."

She nodded, sensing the shift in the atmosphere. "I'm listening."

Papa led her to the stone table, and they both sat down on the cool surface, their legs dangling off the edge. He took a deep breath, His eyes meeting hers with a seriousness that made her heart skip a beat.

"There will come a time—a time called Jacob's Trouble—when there will be a great famine in the land. Not a famine of bread or water, but a famine for hearing the word of the Lord – my Word."

Adeline felt a chill run down her spine, the weight of His words settling in her chest. "Jacob's Trouble," she repeated, the phrase feeling heavy and ominous.

Papa nodded, His gaze unwavering. "Yes. It was spoken of by the prophet Amos. The time is coming sooner than you would care to believe. The Word of the Lord will be scarce, and people will seek it desperately but find it nowhere."

Adeline's mind raced as she tried to process the gravity of what He was saying. She thought of the people she knew, the ones she loved, and the many more she had yet to meet. "What should we do, Papa? How can we prepare?"

Papa's gaze was steady, filled with a depth of wisdom that spanned ages. "Store up my Word in your hearts and minds. Let it become a part of you, so that when the time comes, you can stand firm in the truth. This is part of the call given to Mirabelle, to share the good news with all who would receive it."

Adeline took a deep breath, the enormity of their task settling in her heart. "And what about the scrolls? Should we share them?"

Papa's smile returned, warm and encouraging. "Yes, but more importantly, let their wisdom guide you. There's also something else you must remember. The passages in Matthew that speak of fleeing to the Judean mountains—they are not just for those in the past, but a warning for those in the future. These scrolls have been hidden here and not found, because they are here for the time of trouble. I know it's difficult to understand right now, but there will come a time when having Bibles, even those on your phone, will be illegal. There is coming a day when all Bibles found, will be torched and gotten rid of. In this time, you will need to be as wise as serpents and as harmless as doves."

Adeline's mind whirled with the implications of His words. She knew the passages He was referring to—how the people of

Jerusalem were told to flee to the mountains when they saw the abomination of desolation spoken of by the prophet Daniel. It was a warning that had echoed through history, and now it was a warning for the future.

She felt a sense of urgency, a need to prepare, but also a deep gratitude for this moment—this time alone with Papa, where they could speak openly and honestly about what was to come.

But as serious as the conversation was, there was still a lightness in the air, a sense of camaraderie that she cherished. She looked at Papa, a mischievous smile tugging at her lips.

"So, are you telling me I need to start memorizing all of Isaiah, Jeremiah, and the minor prophets? Because that's a lot of scrolls."

Papa laughed, a deep, rich sound that filled the chamber and warmed her heart. "Well, I wouldn't say you need to memorize all of them, but it wouldn't hurt to get familiar with the highlights."

Adeline grinned, feeling a sense of relief in the levity of the moment. "I'll do my best. But you know, it would be easier if you just downloaded it all into my brain."

Papa raised an eyebrow, His smile playful. "Where would the fun be in that? The journey is just as important as the destination, Addie."

She rolled her eyes good-naturedly, though she couldn't help but smile. "I suppose you're right. You usually are."

They shared a laugh, the tension of the previous conversation easing as they allowed themselves to enjoy the moment. It was a reminder that even amid serious matters, there was always room for joy, for laughter, and for the simple pleasure of being together.

After a while, they lapsed into a comfortable silence, both of them lost in thought. Adeline found herself reflecting on the journey that had brought her here—how she had been led to this place, to these scrolls, and to this conversation with Papa.

She knew that their time together was a gift, one that she would treasure for the rest of her life. But she also knew that it was a time of preparation, of learning and growing so that she could be ready for what was to come.

Finally, Papa broke the silence, His voice soft but filled with conviction. "Addie, you have a unique role to play in what is to come. Your journey is not just about discovering hidden treasures or uncovering ancient truths. It's about preparing yourself and those you love for the days ahead."

Adeline looked at Him, her heart swelling with determination. "I understand, Papa. I'll do whatever it takes."

Papa smiled, His eyes shining with pride and affection. "I know you will, Addie. And remember, you're not alone in this. You have Me, and you have those who walk this journey with you. Together, you will be strong."

Adeline nodded, feeling a sense of peace settle over her. She knew that the road ahead would be challenging, but she also knew that she was not walking it alone.

She reached out and took Papa's hand, squeezing it gently. "Thank you, Papa. For everything."

He squeezed her hand in return, His smile warm and reassuring. "Always, Addie. I'm always with you."

They sat together in the chamber for a while longer, simply enjoying each other's presence. There was no rush, no urgency—just the quiet comfort of knowing that they were together, and that they were ready for whatever lay ahead.

As they finally rose to leave, Adeline took one last look at the stone table and the scrolls that lay upon it.

With Papa by her side, she felt a strength and a courage that filled her heart with hope. And as they walked out of the chamber and into the unknown, she couldn't help but smile, knowing that she was exactly where she was meant to be.

But as they stepped into the corridor, a faint, almost imperceptible sound reached their ears. It was a soft whisper, like the rustling of leaves in the wind, yet it carried with it a weight that made Adeline pause.

Papa stopped, His gaze turning toward the source of the sound, His expression serene yet knowing. The air around them seemed to shift, growing still, and the light from the torches flickered slightly, as if acknowledging an unseen presence.

"Did you hear that?" Adeline asked, her voice tinged with curiosity rather than fear.

Papa nodded, a gentle smile playing on His lips. "I did, Addie. It seems we're being called to another discovery."

Adeline's heart quickened, a mixture of anticipation and wonder filling her. "What is it?"

He looked at her with eyes full of wisdom and compassion, His voice calm and steady. "It's a reminder, my dear one. A reminder that our journey has many layers, and not all of them have been revealed yet."

The whisper grew slightly louder, still gentle but now more distinct, as if beckoning them forward. Adeline felt a thrill of excitement mixed with a sense of reverence.

"Shall we?" Papa asked, offering His hand with a twinkle in His eye that spoke of both the gravity and the joy of what lay ahead.

She took His hand without hesitation, her heart filled with trust. Together, they moved deeper into the labyrinth of tunnels, the sound guiding them like a thread of destiny woven into the fabric of time.

As they walked, the whispers began to form words, ancient and melodic, echoing through the corridors of stone. Adeline couldn't quite make out what they were saying, but the tone was clear—it was a call, an invitation to uncover something hidden, something that had waited for this moment.

Papa squeezed her hand gently, His voice soft and reassuring. "What you are about to see, Addie, will be a glimpse into a truth that has long been concealed. It's something I've prepared for you to discover."

Adeline felt a shiver of anticipation, knowing that whatever was waiting for them would be extraordinary. "I'm ready," she whispered, her voice filled with determination.

Papa smiled, a look of deep affection and pride in His eyes. "I know you are."

They continued down the winding passage, the whispers growing clearer, guiding them toward an unknown destination. Adeline's heart pounded with a mix of excitement and curiosity, her mind racing with possibilities.

Finally, they reached a heavy wooden door, its surface carved with intricate designs that seemed to pulse with a life of their own. The whispers were strongest here, wrapping around the door like a shroud of mystery.

Papa released her hand and stepped forward, placing His palm against the door. The carvings glowed softly under His touch, and with a creak, the door slowly swung open, revealing a chamber bathed in an ethereal light.

Adeline stepped forward, her breath catching as she saw what lay inside. But before she could fully take it in, the door closed softly behind them, sealing them within.

And in the stillness of that sacred space, a voice—clearer now—spoke directly to her heart.

"Welcome, Adeline. You have been chosen to bear witness."

Her pulse quickened, her thoughts racing. What had she been chosen to witness? What truths awaited her in this hidden chamber, and how would they shape the journey still to come?

As the light in the room began to shift and reveal more of the chamber's contents, Adeline knew one thing for certain: whatever lay ahead, it would change her life forever.

But was she truly ready for the revelation that awaited her?

Only time would tell.

27

The Revelation

The chamber was unlike anything Adeline had ever seen. Bathed in a soft, ethereal light that seemed to emanate from the very walls, the room felt alive with an ancient presence. The air was thick with a sense of anticipation, as if the stones themselves were holding their breath, waiting for the moment of revelation.

Adeline stood in the centre of the chamber, her eyes wide with wonder. The floor beneath her feet was smooth, polished to a reflective sheen, and the walls were adorned with intricate carvings that seemed to tell a story—a story she was only beginning to understand.

Papa stood beside her, His presence calm and steady, yet she could sense the gravity of what was about to unfold. He looked at her with a mixture of affection and solemnity, His eyes conveying both the depth of His love and the importance of what she was about to witness.

"Adeline," He began, His voice gentle but firm, "this place has been prepared for you, and for those who will come after you. It holds a truth that has been hidden for ages, waiting for the right moment to be revealed."

Adeline felt a shiver of anticipation run down her spine. "What truth, Papa? What is this place?"

Papa gestured to the walls, where the carvings seemed to shift and move, as if coming to life. "These carvings tell the story of My people, their journey through time, and the covenant I made with them. It is a story of faith, of trials and tribulations, of promises kept and yet to be fulfilled."

Adeline stepped closer to the wall, drawn by the intricate carvings that seemed to pulse with a life of their own. The stone was cool beneath her fingertips, its surface worn smooth by the passage of time, yet the images etched into it were sharp and clear, as if they had been freshly carved. She traced the lines with a reverence born of awe, her fingers following the curves and angles that formed scenes from a distant past.

The carvings were a tapestry of history, each image telling a story that spanned the centuries. She saw prophets standing tall, their hands raised in fervent proclamation, their faces etched with the solemnity of divine burden. The people of Israel were gathered around them, their expressions a mix of fear, hope, and devotion, their lives shaped by the words of those chosen to speak for God.

Adeline's eyes moved along the wall, taking in the scenes of battles fought and won—great armies clashing on fields of green, warriors with shields raised and swords gleaming, the air thick with the tension of conflict. She could almost hear the clash of metal and the cries of the warriors, feel the earth tremble beneath the weight of history being made. The victories were hard-won, the losses heavy, but each battle was a step in the unfolding plan, a testament to the resilience and faith of a people bound by covenant.

Further along, she saw the construction of the Temple, the great stone blocks being hoisted into place by strong, determined hands. The Temple rose majestically, a symbol of the divine presence dwelling among men, its grandeur capturing the awe of all who beheld it. Adeline could sense the reverence of the builders, their work a labour of love and devotion, each stone laid with the knowledge that they were creating something sacred, something eternal.

But as she continued to study the wall, Adeline's breath caught in her throat. Beyond the familiar scenes of Israel's history, she began to notice images that were less clear, yet strangely recognizable. The lines were more fluid, the details more abstract, as if they depicted events not yet solidified in the fabric of time. These were not just scenes from the past, but glimpses of the future—prophecies that had yet to be fulfilled.

She saw images of desolation and despair, of a world in turmoil. The skies were dark, heavy with the weight of impending doom, and the earth itself seemed to groan under the strain. Cities crumbled into ruins, and nations rose against each other in a conflict that seemed without end. There were scenes of people fleeing in terror, their faces contorted with fear, seeking refuge in the mountains, just as the scriptures had foretold.

But then, amidst the chaos, Adeline's eyes fell upon scenes of unspeakable sorrow. She saw Jerusalem, its majestic walls breached, its sacred Temple desecrated. Roman soldiers swarmed the city like locusts, their armour glinting in the harsh light as they ransacked homes, tore down holy places, and dragged the people of Israel into chains. The city of David, once filled with the sounds of worship and life, was now a place of death and despair. The Jewish people, her people, were scattered to the winds, exiled from the land promised to them, their hearts heavy with the weight of loss.

Adeline's heart ached as the images shifted, showing her the long, dark centuries that followed. Pogroms swept through villages, towns, and cities, leaving devastation in their wake. She saw Jews huddled together in fear, their homes set aflame, their lives destroyed by hatred and violence. The horrors of the Holocaust flashed before her eyes—faces gaunt with starvation, bodies piled in heaps, the smoke of crematoriums rising to the heavens like a bitter offering. The suffering of her people was endless, their cries echoing through the ages.

And yet, amidst the chaos, there were also glimpses of hope. A figure robed in light stood at the centre of it all, His presence commanding, His gaze both fierce and compassionate. Around Him, the nations bowed, and the darkness was pushed back by the brilliance of His coming. It was a vision of the return of the King, of a time when all would be made right, when the promise of redemption would be fulfilled. Her beloved Yeshua.

Adeline's heart raced as she took it all in, the gravity of what she was seeing pressing down on her. These were not just stories from the past; they were a roadmap of what was to come, a glimpse into the days that lay ahead.

"This is the story of the ages," Papa continued, His voice gentle yet resonant with the weight of divine truth. "But it is also the story of what is to come."

He stepped closer, His presence comforting yet powerful, and His eyes held hers with a depth that seemed to see into her very soul.

"The days of Jacob's Trouble," He said, His tone sombre, "the time of tribulation, and the return of the King - Yeshua. These are the events that have been foretold, the moments that will shape the future of My creation. What once was, will be again."

Adeline's eyes widened in horror as the truth of His words sank in. She could feel the weight of the past pressing down on her, the echoes of suffering and loss that had shaped her people's history. The thought of those horrors being repeated, of her people enduring such pain again, was unbearable.

"No!" Adeline cried out, her voice breaking with emotion. "Papa, it can't happen again! Not like that!"

The room seemed to hold its breath, the walls echoing with the weight of her despair. Adeline's heart pounded in her chest, a mix of sorrow and fear surging through her veins. She turned away from the images on the wall, unable to bear the thought of her people enduring such horrors again. Tears welled up in her eyes, threatening to spill over as she clenched her fists in frustration.

She looked back at Papa, her eyes pleading for an answer, for some reassurance that the past would not repeat itself. "There has to be another way," she whispered, her voice trembling. "Please, Papa, tell me there's another way."

Papa's gaze softened, His eyes reflecting the depth of His own sorrow. He understood her pain, her fear, her desire to shield those she loved from the suffering that loomed on the horizon. But there was also a quiet strength in His eyes, a deep resolve that spoke of the unchanging nature of His plan.

"My dear one," He said softly, His voice carrying both sorrow and resolve, "I know it is hard to see, but what must come will come. The path to redemption is not easy, and the trials ahead are part of the refining process for My people. It is through the fire that they will be purified, and through the darkness that the light will shine brightest."

Adeline's shoulders trembled as she absorbed His words, the weight of what was to come settling heavily upon her. She knew deep down that Papa's words were true, but the thought of the suffering that lay ahead still tore at her heart.

Papa's hand rested lightly on her shoulder, grounding her in the moment. "You have been given a glimpse, Addie, so that you might understand the times in which you live, and the role you and your family are called to play. The story is not yet complete, and you have a part in its unfolding."

Adeline nodded, her resolve hardening as the reality of her calling settled over her. "I understand, Papa. I will do what is needed."

He smiled, His expression filled with both pride and love. "I know you will, my dear one. And remember, you have everything you need within you – My Word, My Spirit, and My love. Even in the darkest times, the light of King Yeshua will always shine through. The end of the story is already written, and it is one of victory and redemption."

The light in the chamber grew brighter, illuminating the entire room. Adeline could see now that the carvings covered every surface, telling a continuous story that wrapped around the entire chamber. It was a story of hope, of redemption, of a promise that would one day be fulfilled.

As she turned back to Papa, she noticed something she hadn't seen before—a small alcove in the wall, just to the right of the entrance. Inside the alcove was a stone pedestal, and atop the pedestal sat a single scroll, its edges worn with age, yet the parchment itself seemed untouched by time.

Papa's eyes followed hers, and He nodded toward the alcove. "This scroll is for you, Addie. It contains a message that I have written for you alone."

Adeline felt her heart skip a beat. She stepped forward, her hands trembling slightly as she reached for the scroll. The parchment was cool to the touch, and as she unrolled it, the ancient script seemed to shimmer in the light.

The words were written in a language she didn't recognise, yet somehow, she could understand them. It was as if the meaning was being conveyed directly to her heart, bypassing her mind entirely.

As she read, tears filled her eyes. The message was simple, yet profound—a reminder of her purpose, of the love and strength that surrounded her, and of the promise that no matter what lay ahead, she was never alone.

Papa watched her as she read, His expression one of infinite tenderness. When she finally looked up, her eyes shining with tears, He reached out and gently wiped them away.

"This is My promise to you, Addie," He said softly. "You are My beloved, and I will never leave you. No matter what happens, no matter how dark the days may become, I will be with you, guiding you, protecting you, and loving you."

Adeline felt a peace settle over her, a peace that filled her from the inside out. She knew, without a doubt, that she was exactly where she was meant to be, and that she was ready for whatever lay ahead.

"Thank you, Papa," she whispered, her voice filled with emotion. "I'll do my best to honour this gift, to live out the purpose You've given me."

He smiled, His eyes shining with love. "I know you will, Addie. And remember, I am with you, always."

With those words, the images on the wall seemed to shimmer and fade, returning to the stone from which they had emerged, leaving Adeline with the knowledge that she had been given a gift—a glimpse into the divine narrative that spanned all of time, past, present, and future. And with that knowledge came a responsibility, one that she was now ready to embrace, guided by the One who had called her for such a time as this.

28

The Unveiling

Adeline stood with Papa in the familiar ancient fortress, high above the world, where the sky met the earth and the horizon stretched out endlessly. The stones beneath her feet were cool and solid, grounding her amidst the vastness of the view that spread out before them. From this vantage point, she could see the world in all its beauty and complexity—mountains, deserts, oceans, and forests, each one a thread in the grand tapestry of creation.

Papa stood beside her, His presence warm and comforting, as always. His arm was draped loosely around her shoulders, and she leaned into Him, feeling the deep love that radiated from Him. There was something special about this place, this fortress that seemed to exist outside of time. It had been their meeting place for so many conversations, a sacred space where He had revealed truths to her, where He had guided her through the challenges and mysteries of her journey.

"I can't believe how far we've come," Adeline said softly, gazing out at the world below. "It feels like only yesterday that I was just beginning this adventure, and now... now everything is different."

Papa chuckled, a rich, warm sound that filled the air around them. "My dear Addie, time has a way of surprising us, doesn't it? But look at you now—you've grown so much, learned so much. I'm so proud of you." Adeline smiled up at Him, her heart swelling with love. "It's all because of You, Papa. I couldn't have done any of this without You."

He squeezed her shoulder affectionately. "Oh, I don't know about that. You've had it in you all along. I've just been here to remind you of who you are."

She laughed, the sound light and full of joy. "You always know just what to say, don't You?"

Papa's eyes twinkled with playful mischief. "It's part of the job description, you know."

Adeline leaned her head against His chest, savouring the moment of peace and closeness. It was in these quiet moments with Papa that she felt most at home, most herself. The adventure had been long and filled with surprises, but it was these moments that she cherished most—the times when she could simply be with Him, listening to His stories, soaking in His wisdom.

They stood in comfortable silence for a while, gazing out at the world together. Adeline's thoughts drifted back over the journey she had taken, the incredible experiences that had shaped her and brought her to this place.

"I never imagined my life would turn out like this," she mused, her voice soft. "There were so many twists and turns, so many things I didn't understand at first. But now... now it all makes sense."

Papa nodded, His expression thoughtful. "Life has a way of surprising us, doesn't it? But you've handled it all with grace, my dear one. You've faced every challenge, embraced every mystery, and you've come out stronger for it."

Adeline felt a warmth spread through her chest at His words. "I've learned so much, Papa. About who I am, where I come from... and about You."

He turned to look at her, His gaze filled with love and pride. "And what have you learned, Addie?"

She met His eyes, her heart full of the truth she had discovered. "I've learned that I am never alone. That no matter where I go, You are with me. I've learned that my heritage is rich and deep, and that it's a part of me that I should honour and embrace. I've learned that the battles I've faced have made me stronger, that the mysteries I've uncovered have brought me closer to the truth. And most of all, I've learned that Your love is the foundation of everything."

Papa smiled, a smile that was full of warmth and approval. "You've learned well, my dear one. And there is so much more for you to discover."

Adeline's heart fluttered with anticipation at His words. "More?"

He nodded, His expression turning serious. "Yes, Addie. The journey is far from over. You've uncovered many truths, but there are still secrets hidden in the sands of time—secrets that your family must discover. You've seen only the beginning."

Adeline's thoughts turned to the incredible encounters she had experienced—walking with her angelic guide Te Ata Whetu, laughing and learning with her foremother Nani in the Cook Islands, and battling with demons and ghosts in Scotland. Each experience had been a revelation, a step closer to understanding the deeper mysteries of her life and heritage.

She thought of Yeshua, the way He had touched her heart, fulfilling the longing she had carried for so long. His presence had been the most profound of all, grounding her in a faith that transcended time and space.

And then there was the discovery of Moshe's Tabernacle in the desert sands, a moment that had changed history and deepened her understanding of her Jewish heritage.

Adeline turned to Papa, her eyes wide with realization. "There's something about our family, about our past, yes?"

Papa nodded, His expression gentle. "Yes, my dear one. There are stories left untold, legacies left to be recovered. You've done so much, but there's much more to discover."

Adeline felt a surge of excitement mixed with a sense of reverence. The more she uncovered, the deeper her understanding grew, and yet, the more questions seemed to arise. The mysteries of her family, their history, and the paths they were destined to walk—it was all a part of a greater plan, one that was still unfolding.

Suddenly, a familiar sense of purpose and destiny filled her heart. She had felt it before, during their time in Scotland, when the land had spoken to her, revealing the strength and resilience of her Celtic and Viking roots. It was there again now, stronger than ever, as if the very air around them was charged with anticipation.

Papa's voice broke through her thoughts, filled with both warmth and gravity. "There is one more thing, Addie."

She turned to Him, her heart pounding with the weight of His words. "What is it, Papa?"

He gazed out over the horizon, His expression thoughtful. "Your father, Drew—he carries within him a legacy that reaches back through the centuries. There is more to his story, to your family's story, than you yet know."

Adeline's heart skipped a beat. Her father—Drew had been with her every step of the way, a steady and reassuring presence, but she had always sensed there was more to him than met the eye. The way he spoke of their ancestors, the reverence he held for their history—it all hinted at something deeper, something that had yet to be revealed.

"What kind of legacy?" she asked, her voice tinged with curiosity and anticipation.

Papa turned to her, His eyes filled with love and a hint of mystery. "A legacy that ties you to the land of your forefathers. A legacy that reaches back to a time of kings and warriors, of battles fought and won. It's time for Drew to uncover the truths that have been hidden for centuries. It's time for him to step into his place in the story."

As He spoke, a vision flashed before Adeline's eyes—an image of her father standing in a mist-shrouded glen in Scotland, his hand resting on a weathered sword embedded in the earth. The sword gleamed with a faint light, as if it held the secrets of a forgotten time. Behind him, the shadowy figure of a warrior in a tattered cloak emerged, a crown of iron upon his brow. The name whispered through the air, as if carried on the breath of the ages: Robert the Bruce.

Adeline's eyes snapped open, her breath catching in her throat. The vision was vivid, powerful, and it sent a shiver down her spine. There was more to their story—much more. And it was Drew's turn to uncover the truths that had been hidden for centuries.

***

No longer in the fortress, but back in the desert sands alongside her family, Addie turned to her father, her heart pounding with a mix of excitement and anticipation. "Abba, there's something you need to see," she whispered, her voice trembling with the weight of the revelation.

Drew looked at her, his brow furrowing in concern. "What is it, Addie?"

She stepped closer, her voice low but urgent. "It's about Robert the Bruce. There's something—something in our blood, in our history. We need to go back to Scotland. There's a legacy waiting for you there, something that ties us to him."

His eyes widened, and she could see the understanding dawning in his expression. "Scotland? Robert the Bruce?" he echoed, the words heavy with the promise of what was to come.

Adeline nodded, her heart filled with a sense of purpose. "Yes, Abba. The journey isn't over. We've uncovered so much, but there's more—much more. And it's your turn to lead us there."

Drew's gaze turned toward the horizon, where the sun was sinking into the sands, casting the world in shades of gold and crimson. The air was thick with the scent of adventure, of stories yet to be told.

He smiled, a look of determination settling on his face. "Then we go back to Scotland," he said, his voice filled with resolve. "Let's see what the future holds."

Adeline felt a thrill of anticipation as her father's words echoed in the desert air.

Papa's voice filled her mind once more, this time with a note of finality. "The past has led you here, but the future is calling. It's time to uncover the legacy that binds you to the land of your forefathers."

Adeline turned to Yeshua, who had been quietly watching, His presence a constant source of strength. "It's time, Addie," He said, His voice filled with both encouragement and expectation. "The next chapter awaits."

Adeline looked around at her family and friends, at the faces she loved so dearly, each one marked by the journey they had taken together. They were ready—ready to face whatever lay ahead, to uncover the secrets of their past and to forge their future.

"Let's go," she said, her voice filled with confidence. "To Scotland, and to the heart of our legacy."

As they began to move, the desert seemed to come alive with the promise of what was to come. The sands shifted beneath their feet, and the sky above them darkened with the onset of night. But in Adeline's heart, there was a light—a guiding flame that would lead them to the truth, to the legacy of Robert the Bruce, and to the destiny that awaited them all.

Epilogue

The Full Vision

Raibeart Bruis - Robert The Bruce

As Papa spoke, Adeline's vision shifted, and the ancient fortress dissolved around her. She found herself standing in a mist-shrouded glen in Scotland, the air thick with fog that muffled all sound and veiled the landscape in mystery. The ground was soft beneath her feet, damp with dew, and the scent of earth and moss filled the air.

In the heart of the glen stood her stepfather, Drew. He looked familiar but somehow different—there was a weight to his stance, a sense of purpose that went beyond the man she had always known. His hand rested on the hilt of a weathered sword, half-buried in the soil as though it had waited for centuries for this very moment. The sword was ancient, its once-bright blade dulled by time, but as Drew's fingers closed around the handle, a faint glow pulsed from deep within the metal.

The light grew stronger, illuminating the mist around him with a soft, golden hue. It wasn't just the dawn breaking—it was something more. The sword, long dormant, was awakening to Drew's touch, and with it came a stirring in the air, as if history itself was holding its breath.

Adeline stood at a distance, watching her stepfather, feeling the significance of the moment. She could sense something approaching, something powerful and ancient. The mist began to part, and from its depths, a figure emerged—tall and imposing, cloaked in shadow. His mantle was tattered and worn, yet it carried with it the weight of a king. Beneath the cloak, the faint glint of chainmail shimmered, and atop his brow sat a crown, tarnished with age but still commanding respect.

The figure stepped closer to Drew, and though his face remained obscured by the mist, Adeline could feel his presence—strong, wise, and filled with the authority of ages past. This was no ordinary man; this was a king, a warrior, someone who had carried the weight of a nation on his shoulders.

The air thrummed with energy as the figure drew near, the ground beneath Drew trembling as though it, too, recognized the importance of what was happening. Adeline could hear a name whispered on the wind, soft yet unmistakable: "Robert the Bruce."

The name echoed through the glen, carrying with it centuries of history, battles fought for freedom, and a legacy that had endured through the ages. Drew stood still, his hand firmly gripping the sword, as the light from the blade grew brighter, illuminating both the figure before him and the path that lay ahead.

Adeline's heart raced as she watched her stepfather, knowing that this was his moment. The sword in his hand was more than a relic—it was a symbol of the legacy he was now being called to bear. The light from the blade seemed to pulse in time with his heartbeat, as though it recognized him, as though it had been waiting for this moment as much as he had.

The figure, now standing just a breath away from Drew, extended a hand. He didn't speak, but his gesture was clear. This was an offering, a passing of the torch, a call to step into the legacy that had been waiting for him.

Adeline felt the energy crackling in the air, the weight of history pressing in on all sides. She wasn't a part of this moment —she was an observer, witnessing something that had been destined for her beloved stepfather alone. This was his calling, his time to rise.

"The legacy is yours to claim," Robert the Bruce's voice finally spoke, low and filled with the power of ages. "What was lost can be found again. The blood of kings flows in your veins, and now is the time to awaken the truth."

The words settled over the glen like a sacred vow. Drew's hand tightened on the sword, the light within it flaring with a brilliance that lit up the misty landscape. He didn't need to say anything—Adeline could see the resolve in his eyes, the acceptance of the burden and the responsibility that came with it.

This wasn't just about uncovering a forgotten history; it was about stepping into his rightful place, reclaiming what had been lost, and fulfilling a destiny that had been waiting for him through the generations. Drew's lineage, the blood of kings, called to him now, and he was ready to answer.

As the vision began to fade, the figure of Robert the Bruce, the misty glen, and the glowing sword dissolved into the background, leaving only the golden light of the sword pulsing like a heartbeat in the darkness.

With a blink, Adeline was back in the ancient fortress, her heart still racing from what she had witnessed. She looked at Papa, the vision lingering in her mind like an echo of what was to come. Drew's time had come to answer the call of his lineage. The legacy of Robert the Bruce, the ancient sword, and the blood of kings were all real, waiting to be awakened.

This was only the beginning. Adeline knew that her stepfather's journey—indeed, their family's journey—had only just begun. The sword had chosen its heir, and Drew was now bound to a legacy far greater than himself.

The call to reclaim what was lost now lay before Drew, but would he fully embrace the legacy of his ancestors? As Adeline stood watching, she couldn't help but wonder—was her stepfather truly ready to face the challenges that awaited him, to step into the ancient lineage that ran through his veins, and to wield the power of a king? Only time would reveal if Drew would rise to meet his destiny, or if the weight of history would prove too great.

About The Author

Sandi Wilson is, above all, a devoted child of God, a loving wife and mother, a cherished Safta (nana), a devoted daughter, a sister, and a loyal friend. Additionally, she is a passionate author, blogger, and writer.

Her deep-seated love for words has been a constant companion throughout her life, a love she's nurtured since as far back as she can remember. Although her writing journey began with her widely followed blog, Sandi took a significant leap when she directed her creative energy towards her first novel. To her surprise, her work garnered the attention of a prominent publisher in the United Kingdom. While the experience was enlightening, the hurdles of time zones, distance, and a lack of communication prompted Sandi to realise the potential of self-publishing from the comfort of her home. After securing her rights, she bravely ventured into self-publishing.

After the success of her book on Dementia and extensive interviews, Sandi decided to establish her own independent publishing label. Under this label, she is diligently crafting the rest of the seven instalments of her enchanting series, "The Mirabelle Chronicles," alongside a collection of stand-alone stories.

When she's not immersed in the world of writing, Sandi finds immense joy in spending quality time with her cherished family, exploring new destinations, indulging in the pages of captivating books, and delving deeper into her interests in history, archaeology, genealogy, and gardening. Sandi Wilson's multi-faceted life and unwavering passion for storytelling make her an author worth watching as she continues to captivate readers with her words.

Sandi's website: www.skwpublishing.com
Sandi's book site: www.sandikwilson.com

Milton Keynes UK
Ingram Content Group UK Ltd.
UKHW021117111124
451035UK00016B/1076